2001
a space odyssey

2001

a space odyssey

a novel by
Arthur C. Clarke

based on the screenplay by
**Arthur C. Clarke &
Stanley Kubrick**

 **Arrow Books**

Arrow Books Ltd
3 Fitzroy Square, London W1

An imprint of the Hutchinson Publishing Group

London Melbourne Sydney Auckland
Wellington Johannesburg and agencies
throughout the world

First published by Hutchinson & Co. (Publishers) Ltd 1968
Arrow edition 1968
Reprinted 1968, 1970 twice, 1971, 1972, 1973 twice, 1974,
1976, 1978 and 1981
© Arthur C. Clarke and Polaris Productions Inc. 1968

Made and printed in Great Britain
by The Anchor Press Ltd
Tiptree, Essex

ISBN 0 09 906610 6

Contents

Foreword

Behind every man now alive stand thirty ghosts, for that is the ratio by which the dead outnumber the living. Since the dawn of time, roughly a hundred billion human beings have walked the planet Earth.

Now this is an interesting number, for by a curious coincidence there are approximately a hundred billion stars in our local universe, the Milky Way. So for every man who has ever lived, in this universe, there shines a star.

But every one of those stars is a sun, often far more brilliant and glorious than the small, nearby star we call *the* Sun. And many—perhaps most—of those alien suns have planets circling them. So almost certainly there is enough land in the sky to give every member of the human species, back to the first ape-man, his own private, world-sized heaven—or hell.

How many of those potential heavens and hells are now inhabited, and by what manner of creatures, we have no way of guessing; the very nearest is a million times further away than Mars or Venus, those still remote goals of the next generation. But the barriers of distance are crumbling; one day we shall meet our equals, or our masters, among the stars.

Men have been slow to face this prospect; some still hope that it may never become reality. Increasing numbers, however, are asking: 'Why have such meetings not occurred already, since we ourselves are about to venture into space?'

Why not, indeed? Here is one possible answer to that very reasonable question. But please remember: this is only a work of fiction.

The truth, as always, will be far stranger.

A.C.C.

S.K.

I

PRIMEVAL NIGHT

1

The Road to Extinction

The drought had lasted now for ten million years, and the reign of the terrible lizards had long since ended. Here on the Equator, in the continent which would one day be known as Africa, the battle for existence had reached a new climax of ferocity, and the victor was not yet in sight. In this barren and desiccated land only the small or the swift or the fierce could flourish, or even hope to survive.

The man-apes of the veldt were none of these things, and they were not flourishing; indeed, they were already far down the road to racial extinction. About fifty of them occupied a group of caves overlooking a small, parched valley, which was divided by a sluggish stream fed from snows in the mountains two hundred miles to the north. In bad times the stream vanished completely, and the tribe lived in the shadow of thirst.

It was always hungry, and now it was starving. When the first faint glow of dawn crept into the cave Moon-Watcher saw that his father had died in the night. He did not know that the Old One was his father, for such a relationship was utterly beyond his understanding, but as he looked at the emaciated body he felt a dim disquiet that was the ancestor of sadness.

The two babies were already whimpering for food, but became silent when Moon-Watcher snarled at them. One of the mothers, defending the infant she could not properly feed, gave him an angry growl in return; he lacked the energy even to cuff her for her presumption.

Now it was light enough to leave. Moon-Watcher picked up the shrivelled corpse, and dragged it after him as he bent under the low overhang of the cave. Once outside, he threw the body over his shoulder and stood upright—the only animal in all this world able to do so.

Among his kind, Moon-Watcher was almost a giant. He was nearly five feet high, and though badly undernourished weighed over a hundred pounds. His hairy, muscular body was half-way between ape and man, but his head was already much nearer to man than ape. The forehead was low, and there were ridges over the eye-sockets, yet he unmistakably held in his genes the promise of humanity. As he looked out upon the hostile world of the Pleistocene there was already something in his gaze beyond the capacity of any ape. In those dark, deep-set eyes was a dawning awareness—the first intimations of an intelligence that could not possibly fulfil itself for ages yet, and might soon be extinguished for ever.

There was no sign of danger, so Moon-Watcher began to scramble down the almost vertical slope outside the cave, only slightly hindered by his burden. As if they had been waiting for his signal, the rest of the tribe emerged from their own homes further down the rock-face, and began to hasten towards the muddy waters of the stream for their morning drink.

Moon-Watcher looked across the valley to see if the Others were in sight, but there was no trace of them. Perhaps they had not yet left their caves, or were already foraging further along the hillside. Since they were nowhere to be seen, Moon-Watcher forgot them; he was incapable of worrying about more than one thing at a time.

First he must get rid of the Old One, but this was a problem that demanded little thought. There had been many deaths this season, one of them in his own cave; he had only to put the corpse where he had left the new baby at the last quarter of the moon, and the hyenas would do the rest.

They were already waiting, where the little valley fanned out into the savannah, almost as if they had known that he was coming. Moon-Watcher left the body under a small bush—all the earlier bones had already gone—and hurried back to rejoin the tribe. He never thought of his father again.

His two mates, the adults from the other caves, and most of the youngsers were foraging among the drought-stunted trees further up the valley, looking for berries, succulent roots and leaves, and occasional windfalls like small lizards or rodents. Only the babies and the feeblest of the old folk were left in the caves; if there was any surplus food at the end of the day's searching they might be fed. If not, the hyenas would soon be in luck once more.

But this day was a good one—though as Moon-Watcher had no real remembrance of the past, he could not compare one time with another. He had found a hive of bees in the stump of a dead tree, and so had enjoyed the finest delicacy that his people could ever know; he still licked his fingers from time to time as he led the group homewards in the late afternoon. Of course, he had also collected a fair number of stings, but he had scarcely noticed them. He was now as near to contentment as he was ever likely to be; for though he was still hungry, he was not actually weak with hunger. That was the most for which any man-ape could ever aspire.

His contentment vanished when he reached the stream. The Others were there. They were there every day, but that did not make it any the less annoying.

There were about thirty of them, and they could not have been distinguished from the members of Moon-Watcher's own tribe. As they saw him coming they began to dance, shake their arms, and shriek on their side of the stream, and his own people replied in kind.

And that was all that happened. Though the man-apes often fought and wrestled among each other, their disputes very seldom resulted in serious injuries. Having no claws or fighting canines, and being well protected by hair, they could not inflict much harm on one another. In any event, they had little surplus energy for such unproductive behaviour; snarling and threatening was a much more efficient way of asserting their points of view.

The confrontation lasted about five minutes; then the display died out as quickly as it had begun, and everyone drank his fill of the muddy water. Honour had been satisfied; each group had staked its claim to its own territory. This important business having been settled, the tribe moved off along its side of the river. The nearest worthwhile grazing was now more than a mile from the caves, and they had to share it with a herd of large, antelope-like beasts who barely tolerated their presence. They could not be driven away, for they were armed with ferocious daggers on their foreheads— the natural weapons which the man-apes did not possess.

So Moon-Watcher and his companions chewed berries and fruit and leaves and fought off the pangs of hunger— while all around them, competing for the same fodder, was a potential source of more food than they could ever hope to eat. Yet the thousands of tons of succulent meat roaming over the savannah and through the bush was not only beyond their reach; it was beyond their imagination. In the midst of plenty they were slowly starving to death.

The tribe returned to its cave without incident, in the last light of the day. The injured female who had remained behind cooed with pleasure as Moon-Watcher gave her the berry-covered branch he had brought back, and began to attack it ravenously. There was little enough nourishment here, but it would help her to survive until the wound the leopard had given her had healed, and she could forage for herself again.

Over the valley, a full moon was rising, and a chill wind was blowing down from the distant mountains. It would be very cold tonight—but cold, like hunger, was not a matter for any real concern; it was merely part of the background of life.

Moon-Watcher barely stirred when the shrieks and screams echoed up the slope from one of the lower caves, and he did not need to hear the occasional growl of the leopard to know exactly what was happening. Down there in the darkness old White Hair and his family were fighting and dying, and the thought that he might help in some way never crossed Moon-Watcher's mind. The harsh logic of survival ruled out such fancies, and not a voice was raised in protest from the listening hillside. Every cave was silent, lest it also attract disaster.

The tumult died away, and presently Moon-Watcher could hear the sound of a body being dragged over the rocks. That lasted only a few seconds; then the leopard got a good hold on its kill. It made no further noise as it padded silently away, carrying its victim effortlessly in its jaws.

For a day or two there would be no further danger here, but there might be other enemies abroad, taking advantage of this cold Little Sun that shone only by night. If there was sufficient warning the smaller predators would sometimes be scared away by shouts and screams. Moon-Watcher crawled out of the cave, clambered on to a large boulder beside the entrance, and squatted there to survey the valley.

Of all the creatures who had yet walked on Earth, the man-apes were the first to look steadfastly at the Moon. And though he could not remember it, when he was very young Moon-Watcher would sometimes reach out and try to touch that ghostly face rising above the hills.

He had never succeeded, and now he was old enough to understand why. For first, of course, he must find a high enough tree to climb.

Sometimes he watched the valley, and sometimes he watched the Moon, but always he listened. Once or twice he dozed off, but he slept with a hair-trigger alertness, and the slightest sound would have disturbed him. At the great age of twenty-five he was still in full possession of all his faculties; if his luck continued, and he avoided accidents, disease, predators and starvation, he might survive for as much as another ten years.

The night wore on, cold and clear, without further alarms, and the Moon rose slowly amid equatorial constellations that no human eye would ever see. In the caves, between spells of fitful dozing and fearful waiting, were being born the nightmares of generations yet to be.

And twice there passed slowly across the sky, rising up to the zenith and descending into the east, a dazzling point of light more brilliant than any star.

2

The New Rock

Late that night Moon-Watcher suddenly awoke. Tired out by the day's exertions and disasters, he had been sleeping more soundly than usual, yet he was instantly alert at the first faint scrabbling down in the valley.

He sat up in the fetid darkness of the cave, straining his senses out into the night, and fear crept slowly into his soul. Never in his life—already twice as long as most members of his species could expect—had he heard a sound like this. The great cats approached in silence, and the only thing that betrayed them was a rare slide of earth, or the occasional cracking of a twig. Yet this was a continuous crunching noise that grew steadily louder. It seemed that some enormous beast was moving through the night, making no attempt at concealment, and ignoring all obstacles. Once Moon-Watcher heard the unmistakable sound of a bush being uprooted; the elephants and dinotheria did this often enough, but otherwise they moved as silently as the cats.

And then there came a sound which Moon-Watcher could not possibly have identified, for it had never been heard before in the history of the world. It was the clank of metal upon stone.

.   .   .   .   .

Moon-Watcher came face to face with the New Rock when he led the tribe down to the river in the first light of morning. He had almost forgotten the terrors of the night, because nothing had happened after that initial noise, so he did not even associate this strange thing with danger or with fear. There was, after all, nothing in the least alarming about it.

It was a rectangular slab, three times his height but narrow enough to span with his arms, and it was made of some completely transparent material; indeed, it was not easy to see except when the rising sun glinted on its edges. As Moon-Watcher had never encountered ice, or even crystal-clear water, there were no natural object to which he could compare this apparition. It was certainly rather attractive, and though he was wisely cautious of most new things, he did not hesitate for long before sidling up to it. As nothing happened, he put out his hand, and felt a cold, hard surface.

After several minutes of intense thought he arrived at a brilliant explanation. It was a rock, of course, and it must have grown during the night. There were many plants that did this—white, pulpy things shaped like pebbles, that seemed to shoot up during the hours of darkness. It was true that they were small and round, whereas this was large and sharp-edged; but greater and later philosophers than Moon-Watcher would be prepared to overlook equally striking exceptions to their theories.

This really superb piece of abstract thinking led Moon-

Watcher, after only three or four minutes, to a deduction
which he immediately put to the test. The white, round
pebble-plants were very tasty (though there were a few that
produced violent illness), perhaps this tall one . . .?

A few licks and nibbles quickly disillusioned him. There
was no nourishment here; so like a sensible man-ape, he
continued on his way to the river and forgot all about the
crystalline monolith during the daily routine of shrieking at
the Others.

The foraging today was very bad, and the tribe had to
travel several miles from the caves to find any food at all.
During the merciless heat of noon, one of the frailer females
collapsed, far from any possible shelter. Her companions
gathered round her, twittering and weeping sympathetically,
but there was nothing that anyone could do. If they had been
less exhausted they might have carried her with them, but
there was no surplus energy for such acts of kindness. She
had to be left behind, to recover or not with her own
resources.

They passed the spot on the homeward trek that evening;
there was not a bone to be seen.

In the last light of day, looking round anxiously for early
hunters, they drank hastily at the stream and started the
climb up to their caves. They were still a hundred yards
from the New Rock when the sound began.

It was barely audible, yet it stopped them dead, so that
they stood paralysed on the trail with their jaws hanging
slackly. A simple, maddeningly repetitive vibration, it
pulsed out from the crystal, and hypnotised all who came
within its spell. For the first time—and the last, for three
million years—the sound of drumming was heard in Africa.

The throbbing grew louder, more insistent. Presently the
man-apes began to move forward like sleep-walkers towards
the source of that compulsive sound. Sometimes they took
little dancing steps, as their blood responded to rhythms that
their descendants would not create for ages yet. Totally

entranced, they gathered round the monolith, forgetting the hardships of the day, the perils of the approaching dusk, and the hunger in their bellies.

The drumming became louder, the night darker. And as the shadows lengthened, and the light drained from the sky, the crystal began to glow.

First it lost its transparency, and became suffused with a pale, milky luminescence. Tantalising, ill-defined phantoms moved across its surface and in its depths. They coalesced into bars of light and shadow, then formed intermeshing, spoked patterns that began slowly to rotate.

Faster and faster spun the wheels of light, and the throbbing of the drums accelerated with them. Now utterly hypnotised, the man-apes could only stare slack-jawed into this astonishing display of pyrotechnics. They had already forgotten the instincts of their forefathers and the lessons of a lifetime; not one of them, ordinarily, would have been so far from his cave, so late in the evening, for the surrounding brush was full of frozen shapes and staring eyes, as the creatures of the night suspended their business to see what would happen next.

Now the spinning wheels of light began to merge, and the spokes fused into luminous bars that slowly receded into the distance, rotating on their axes as they did so. They split into pairs, and the resulting sets of lines started to oscillate across each other, slowly changing their angles of intersection. Fantastic, fleeting geometrical patterns flickered in and out of existence as the glowing grids meshed and unmeshed; and the man-apes watched, mesmerised captives of the shining crystal.

They could never guess that their minds were being probed, their bodies mapped, their reactions studied, their potentials evaluated. At first the whole tribe remained half crouching in a motionless tableau, as if frozen into stone. Then the man-ape nearest to the slab suddenly came to life.

He did not move from his position, but his body lost its trance-like rigidity, and became animated as if it were a puppet controlled by invisible strings. The head turned this way and that; the mouth silently opened and closed; the hands clenched and unclenched. Then he bent down, snapped off a long stalk of grass, and attempted to tie it into a knot with clumsy fingers.

He seemed to be a thing possessed, struggling against some spirit or demon who had taken over control of his body. He was panting for breath, and his eyes were full of terror as he tried to force his fingers to make movements more complex than any that they had ever attempted before.

Despite all his efforts, he succeeded only in breaking the stalk into pieces. As the fragments fell to the ground, the controlling influence left him, and he froze once more into immobility.

Another man-ape came to life, and went through the same routine. This was a younger, more adaptable specimen: it succeeded where the older one had failed. On the planet Earth the first crude knot had been tied. . . .

Others did stranger and still more pointless things. Some held their hands out at arm's-length, and tried to touch their fingertips together—first with both eyes open, then with one closed. Some were made to stare at ruled patterns in the crystal, that became more and more finely divided until the lines had merged into a grey blur. And all heard single pure sounds, of varying pitch, that swiftly sank below the level of hearing.

When Moon-Watcher's turn came he felt very little fear. His main sensation was a dull resentment, as his muscles twitched and his limbs moved at commands that were not wholly his own.

Without knowing why, he bent down and picked up a small stone. When he straightened up he saw that there was a new image in the crystal slab.

The grids and the moving, dancing patterns had gone.

Instead, there was a series of concentric circles, surrounding a small black disc.

Obeying the silent orders in his brain, he pitched the stone with a clumsy, overarm throw. It missed the target by several feet.

Try again, said the command. He searched around until he had found another pebble. This time it hit the slab with a ringing, bell-like tone. He was still a long way off, but his aim was improving.

At the fourth attempt he was only inches from the central bull's-eye. A feeling of indescribable pleasure, almost sexual in its intensity, flooded his mind. Then the control relaxed; he felt no impulse to do anything, except to stand and wait.

One by one, every member of the tribe was briefly possessed. Some succeeded, but most failed at the tasks they had been set, and all were appropriately rewarded by spasms of pleasure or of pain.

Now there was only a uniform, featureless glow in the great slab, so that it stood like a block of light superimposed on the surrounding darkness. As if waking from a sleep, the man-apes shook their heads, and presently began to move along the trail to their place of shelter. They did not look back, or wonder at the strange light that was guiding them to their homes—and to a future unknown, as yet, even to the stars.

3

Academy

Moon-Watcher and his companions had no recollection of what they had seen after the crystal had ceased to cast its hypnotic spell over their minds and to experiment with their bodies. The next day, as they went out to forage, they passed it with scarcely a second thought: it was now part of the disregarded background of their lives. They could not eat it, and it could not eat them; therefore it was not important.

Down at the river the Others made their usual ineffectual threats. Their leader, a one-eared man-ape of Moon-Watcher's size and age, but in poorer condition, even made a brief foray towards the tribe's territory, screaming loudly and waving his arms in an attempt to scare the opposition and to bolster his own courage. The water of the stream was nowhere more than a foot deep, but the further One-Ear moved out into it, the more uncertain and unhappy he became. Very soon he slowed to a halt, and then moved back, with exaggerated dignity, to join his companions.

Otherwise, there was no change in the normal routine. The tribe gathered just enough nourishment to survive for another day, and no one died.

And that night the crystal slab was still waiting, surrounded by its pulsing aura of light and sound. The programme it had contrived, however, was now subtly different. Some of the man-apes it ignored completely, as if it was concentrating on the most promising subjects. One of them was Moon-Watcher; once again he felt inquisitive tendrils creeping down the unused byways of his brain. And presently he began to see visions.

They might have been within the crystal block; they might have been wholly inside his mind. In any event, to Moon-Watcher they were completely real. Yet somehow the usual automatic impulse to drive off invaders of his territory had been lulled into quiescence.

He was looking at a peaceful family group, differing in only one respect from the scenes he knew. The male, female and two infants that had mysteriously appeared before him were gorged and replete, with sleek and glossy pelts—and this was a condition of life that Moon-Watcher had never imagined. Unconsciously, he felt his own protruding ribs;

the ribs of *these* creatures were hidden in rolls of fat. From time to time they stirred lazily, as they lolled at ease near the entrance of a cave, apparently at peace with the world. Occasionally the big male emitted a monumental burp of contentment.

There was no other activity, and after five minutes the scene suddenly faded out. The crystal was no more than a glimmering outline in the darkness; Moon-Watcher shook himself as if awaking from a dream, abruptly realised where he was, and led the tribe back to the caves.

He had no conscious memory of what he had seen, but that night, as he sat brooding at the entrance of his lair, his ears attuned to the noises of the world around him, Moon-Watcher felt the first faint twinges of a new and potent emotion. It was a vague and diffuse sense of envy—of dissatisfaction with his life. He had no idea of its cause, still less of its cure; but discontent had come into his soul, and he had taken one small step towards humanity.

Night after night the spectacle of those four plump man-apes was repeated, until it had become a source of fascinated exasperation, serving to increase Moon-Watcher's eternal, gnawing hunger. The evidence of his eyes could not have produced this effect; it needed psychological reinforcement. There were gaps in Moon-Watcher's life now that he would never remember, when the very atoms of his simple brain were being twisted into new patterns. If he survived, those patterns would become eternal, for his genes would pass them on to future generations.

It was a slow, tedious business, but the crystal monolith was patient. Neither it, nor its replicas scattered across half the globe, expected to succeed with all the scores of groups involved in the experiment. A hundred failures would not matter when a single success could change the destiny of the world.

By the time of the next new moon the tribe had seen one birth and two deaths. One of these had been due to starvation; the other had occurred during the nightly ritual, when a man-ape had suddenly collapsed while attempting to tap two pieces of stone delicately together. At once the crystal had darkened, and the tribe had been released from the spell. But the fallen man-ape had not moved and by the morning, of course, the body was gone.

There had been no performance the next night; the crystal was still analysing its mistake. The tribe streamed past it through the gathering dusk, ignoring its presence completely. The night after, it was ready for them again.

The four plump man-apes were still there, and now they were doing extraordinary things. Moon-Watcher began to tremble uncontrollably; he felt as if his brain would burst, and wanted to turn away his eyes. But that remorseless mental control would not relax its grip; he was compelled to follow the lesson to the end, though all his instincts revolted against it.

Those instincts had served his ancestors well, in the days of warm rains and lush fertility, when food was to be had everywhere for the plucking. Now times had changed, and the inherited wisdom of the past had become folly. The man-apes must adapt, or they must die—like the greater beasts who had gone before them, and whose bones now lay sealed within the limestone hills.

So Moon-Watcher stared at the crystal monolith with unblinking eyes, while his brain lay open to its still uncertain manipulations. Often he felt nausea, but always he felt hunger; and from time to time his hands clenched unconsciously in the patterns that would determine his new way of life.

.   .   .   .   .

As the line of wart-hogs moved snuffling and grunting across the trail, Moon-Watcher came to a sudden halt. Pigs and man-apes had always ignored each other, for there was no conflict of interest between them. Like most animals that did not compete for the same food, they merely kept out of each others' way.

Yet now Moon-Watcher stood looking at them, wavering back and forth uncertainly as he was buffeted by impulses which he could not understand. Then, as if in a dream, he started searching the ground—though for what he could not have explained even if he had the power of speech. He would recognise it when he saw it.

It was a heavy, pointed stone about six inches long, and though it did not fit his hand perfectly, it would do. As he swung his hand around, puzzled by its suddenly increased weight, he felt a pleasing sense of power and authority. He started to move towards the nearest pig.

It was a young and foolish animal, even by the undemanding standards of wart-hog intelligence. Though it observed him out of the corner of its eye, it did not take him seriously until much too late. Why should it suspect these harmless creatures of any evil intent? It went on rooting up the grass until Moon-Watcher's stone hammer obliterated its dim consciousness. The remainder of the herd continued grazing unalarmed, for the murder had been swift and silent.

All the other man-apes in the group had stopped to watch, and now they crowded round Moon-Watcher and his victim with admiring wonder. Presently one of them picked up the blood-stained weapon and began to pound the dead pig. Others joined in with any sticks and stones that they could gather until their target began a messy disintegration.

Then they became bored; some wandered off, while others stood hesitantly around the unrecognisable corpse—the future of a world waiting upon their decision. It was a surprisingly long time before one of the nursing females began to lick the gory stone she was holding in her paws.

And it was longer still before Moon-Watcher, despite all that he had been shown, really understood that he need never be hungry again.

4

The Leopard

The tools they had been programmed to use were simple enough, yet they could change this world and make the man-apes its masters. The most primitive was the hand-held stone, that multiplied many-fold the power of a blow. Then there was the bone club, that lengthened the reach and could provide a buffer against the fangs or claws of angry animals. With these weapons, the limitless food that roamed the savannahs was theirs to take.

But they needed other aids, for their teeth and nails could not readily dismember anything larger than a rabbit. Luckily, Nature had provided the perfect tools, requiring only the wit to pick them up.

First there was a crude but very efficient knife or saw, of a model that would serve well for the next three million years. It was simply the lower jaw-bone of an antelope, with the teeth still in place; there would be no substantial improvement until the coming of steel. Then there was an awl or dagger in the form of a gazelle horn, and finally a scraping tool made from the complete jaw of almost any small animal.

The stone club, the toothed saw, the horn dagger, the bone scraper—these were the marvellous inventions which the man-apes needed to survive. Soon they would recognise them for the symbols of power that they were, but many months must pass before their clumsy fingers had acquired the skill—or the will—to use them.

Perhaps, given time, they might by their own efforts have come to the awesome and brilliant concept of using natural weapons as artificial tools. But the odds were all against them, and even now there were endless opportunities for failure in the ages that lay ahead.

The man-apes had been given their first chance. There would be no second one; the future was, very literally, in their own hands.

.　　　.　　　.　　　.　　　.

Moons waxed and waned; babies were born and sometimes lived; feeble, toothless thirty-year-olds died; the leopard took its toll in the night; the Others threatened daily across the river—and the tribe prospered. In the course of a single year Moon-Watcher and his companions had changed almost beyond recognition.

They had learned their lessons well; now they could handle all the tools that had been revealed to them. The very memory of hunger was fading from their minds; and though the wart-hogs were becoming shy, there were gazelles and antelopes and zebras in countless thousands on the plains. All these animals, and others, had fallen prey to the apprentice hunters.

Now that they were no longer half-numbed with starvation, they had time both for leisure and for the first rudiments of thought. Their new way of life was now casually accepted, and they did not associate it in any way with the monolith still standing beside the trail to the river. If they had ever stopped to consider the matter, they might have boasted that they had brought about their improved status by their own efforts; in fact, they had already forgotten any other mode of existence.

But no Utopia is perfect, and this one had two blemishes. The first was the marauding leopard, whose passion for man-apes seemed to have grown even stronger now that they were better nourished. The second was the tribe across the river; for somehow the Others had survived and had stubbornly refused to die of starvation.

The leopard problem was resolved partly by chance, partly owing to a serious—indeed, almost fatal—error on

Moon-Watcher's part. Yet at the time his idea had seemed such a brilliant one that he had danced with joy, and perhaps he could hardly be blamed for overlooking the consequences.

The tribe still experienced occasional bad days, though these no longer threatened its very survival. Towards dusk it had failed to make a kill; the home caves were already in sight as Moon-Watcher led his tired and disgruntled companions back to shelter. And there, on their very threshold, they found one of Nature's rare bonanzas.

A full-grown antelope was lying by the trail. Its foreleg was broken, but it still had plenty of fight in it, and the circling jackals gave its daggerlike horns a respectful berth. They could afford to wait; they knew that they had only to bide their time.

But they had forgotten about the competition, and retreated with angry snarls when the man-apes arrived. They too circled warily, keeping beyond the range of those dangerous horns; then they moved to the attack with clubs and stones.

It was not a very effective or co-ordinated attack: by the time the wretched beast had been given its quietus the light had almost gone—and the jackals were regaining their courage. Moon-Watcher, torn between fear and hunger, slowly realised that all this effort might have been in vain. It was too dangerous to stay here any longer.

Then, not for the first or the last time, he proved himself a genius. With an immense effort of imagination he visualised the dead antelope—*in the safety of his own cave*. He began to drag it towards the cliff-face; presently, the others understood his intentions, and began to help him.

If he had known how difficult the task would be he would never have attempted it. Only his great strength, and the agility inherited from his arboreal ancestors, allowed him to haul the carcass up the steep slope. Several times, almost weeping with frustration, he almost abandoned his prize, but a stubbornness as deep-seated as his hunger drove him on. Sometimes the others helped him, sometimes they hindered; more often they merely got in the way. But finally it was done; the battered antelope was dragged over the lip of the cave, as the last hues of sunlight faded from the sky; and the feasting began.

Hours later, gorged to repletion, Moon-Watcher awoke. Not knowing why, he sat up in the darkness among the sprawled bodies of his equally satiated companions, and strained his ears into the night.

There was no sound except the heavy breathing around him; the whole world seemed asleep. The rocks beyond the mouth of the cave were pale as bone in the brilliant light from the Moon, now high overhead. Any thought of danger seemed infinitely remote.

Then, from a long way off, came the sound of a falling pebble. Fearful, yet inquisitive, Moon-Watcher crawled out on to the ledge of the cave, and peered down the face of the cliff.

What he saw left him so paralysed with fright that for long seconds he was unable to move. Only twenty feet below, two gleaming golden eyes were staring straight up at him; they held him so hypnotised with fear that he was scarcely aware of the lithe, streaked body behind them, flowing smoothly and silently from rock to rock. Never before had the leopard climbed so high. It had ignored the lower caves, though it must have been well aware of their inhabitants. Now it was after other game; it was following the spoor of blood, up the moon-washed face of the cliff.

Seconds later, the night was made hideous by the shrieks of alarm from the man-apes in the cave above. The leopard gave a snarl of fury, as it realised that it had lost the element of surprise. But it did not check its advance, for it knew that it had nothing to fear.

It reached the ledge, and rested for a moment on the narrow open space. The scent of blood was all around, filling its fierce and tiny mind with one overwhelming desire. Without hesitation, it padded silently into the cave.

And here it made its first error, for as it moved out of the moonlight even its superbly night-adapted eyes were at a momentary disadvantage. The man-apes could see it, partly silhouetted against the opening of the cave, more clearly than it could see them. They were terrified, but they were no longer utterly helpless.

Snarling and lashing its tail in arrogant confidence, the leopard advanced in search of the tender food that it craved. Had it met its prey in the open, it would have had no problems; but now that the man-apes were trapped, desperation had given them the courage to attempt the impossible. And for the first time, they had the means to achieve it.

The leopard knew that something was wrong when it felt a stunning blow on its head. It lashed out with its forepaw, and heard a shriek of agony as its claws slashed through soft flesh. Then there was a piercing pain as something sharp drove into its flanks—once, twice, and yet a third time. It whirled around to strike at the shadows screaming and dancing on all sides.

Again there was a violent blow as something caught it across the snout. Its teeth snapped on a white, moving blur —only to grate uselessly upon dead bone. And now, in a final, unbelievable indignity, its tail was being dragged out by the roots.

It whirled around, throwing its insanely daring tormentor against the wall of the cave. Yet whatever it did, it could not escape the rain of blows, inflicted on it by crude weapons wielded by clumsy but powerful hands. Its snarls ran the gamut from pain to alarm, from alarm to outright terror. The implacable hunter was now the victim, and was desperately trying to retreat.

And then it made its second mistake, for in its surprise and fright it had forgotten where it was. Or perhaps it had been dazed or blinded by the blows rained on its head;

whatever the reason, it bolted abruptly from the cave. There was a horrible screech as it went toppling out into space. Ages later, it seemed, there came a thud as it crashed into an outcropping half-way down the cliff; thereafter, the only sound was the sliding of loose stones, which quickly died away into the night.

For a long time, intoxicated by victory, Moon-Watcher stood dancing and gibbering at the entrance of the cave. He rightly sensed that his whole world had changed, and that he was no longer a powerless victim of the forces around him.

Then he went back into the cave and for the first time in his life had an unbroken night's sleep.

In the morning they found the body of the leopard at the foot of the cliff. Even in death it was some time before anyone dared to approach the vanquished monster, but presently they closed in upon it with their bone knives and saws.

It was very hard work, and they did no hunting that day.

5

Encounter in the Dawn

As he led the tribe down to the river in the dim light of dawn, Moon-Watcher paused uncertainly at a familiar spot. Something, he knew, was missing, but what it was he could not remember. He wasted no mental effort on the problem, for this morning he had more important matters on his mind.

Like thunder and lightning and clouds and eclipses the great block of crystal had departed as mysteriously as it had come. Having vanished into the non-existent past, it never troubled Moon-Watcher's thoughts again.

He would never know what it had done to him; and none of his companions wondered, as they gathered round him in the morning mist, why he had paused for a moment here on the way to the river.

.   .   .   .   .

From their side of the stream, in the never-violated safety of their own territory, the Others first saw Moon-Watcher and a dozen males of his tribe as a moving frieze against the dawn sky. At once they began to scream their daily challenge, but this time there was no answer.

Steadily, purposefully—above all, *silently*—Moon-Watcher and his band descended the low hillock that overlooked the river; and as they approached, the Others became suddenly quiet. Their ritual rage ebbed away, to be replaced by a mounting fear. They were dimly aware that something had happened, and that this encounter was unlike all those that had ever gone before. The bone clubs and knives that Moon-Watcher's group carried did not alarm them, for they did not understand their purpose. They only knew that their rivals' movements were now imbued with determination, and with menace.

The party stopped at the water's edge, and for a moment the Others' courage revived. Led by One-Ear, they half-heartedly resumed their battle-chant. It lasted only a few seconds before a vision of terror struck them dumb.

Moon-Watcher raised his arms high into the air, revealing the burden that until now had been concealed by the hirsute bodies of his companions. He was holding a stout branch, and impaled upon it was the bloody head of the leopard. The mouth had been jammed open with a stick, and the great fangs gleamed a ghastly white in the first rays of the rising sun.

Most of the Others were too paralysed with fright to move, but some began a slow, stumbling retreat. That was all the encouragement that Moon-Watcher needed. Still holding the mangled trophy above his head, he started to cross the stream. After a moment's hesitation, his companions splashed after him.

When Moon-Watcher reached the far side, One-Ear was still standing his ground. Perhaps he was too brave or too stupid to run; perhaps he could not really believe that this outrage was actually happening. Coward or hero, it made no difference in the end, as the frozen snarl of death came crashing down upon his uncomprehending head.

Shrieking with fright, the Others scattered into the bush; but presently they would return, and soon they would forget their lost leader.

For a few seconds Moon-Watcher stood uncertainly above his new victim, trying to grasp the strange and wonderful fact that the dead leopard could kill again. Now he was master of the world, and he was not quite sure what to do next.

But he would think of something.

6

Ascent of Man

A new animal was abroad on the planet, spreading slowly out from the African heartland. It was still so rare that a hasty census might have overlooked it, among the teeming billions of creatures roving over land and sea. There was no evidence, as yet, that it would prosper or even survive: on this world, where so many mightier beasts had passed away, its fate still wavered in the balance.

In the hundred thousand years since the crystals had

descended upon Africa, the man-apes had invented nothing. But they had started to change, and had developed skills which no other animal possessed. Their bone clubs had increased their reach and multiplied their strength; they were no longer defenceless against the predators with whom they had to compete. The smaller carnivores they could drive away from their own kills; the larger ones they could at least discourage, and sometimes put to flight.

Their massive teeth were growing smaller, for they were no longer essential. The sharp-edged stones that could be used to dig out roots, or to cut and saw through tough flesh or fibre, had begun to replace them, with immeasurable consequences. No longer were the man-apes faced with starvation when their teeth became damaged or worn; even the crudest tools could add many years to their lives. And as their fangs diminished, the shape of their face started to alter; the snout receded, the massive jaw became more delicate, the mouth able to make more subtle sounds. Speech was still a million years away, but the first steps towards it had been taken.

And then the world began to change. In four great waves, with two hundred thousand years between their crests, the Ice Ages swept by, leaving their mark on all the globe. Outside the tropics, the glaciers slew those who had prematurely left their ancestral home; and everywhere they winnowed out the creatures who could not adapt.

When the ice had passed, so had much of the planet's early life—including the man-apes. But, unlike so many others, they had left descendants; they had not merely become extinct—they had been transformed. The tool-makers had been remade by their own tools.

For in using clubs and flints their hands had developed a dexterity found nowhere else in the animal kingdom, permitting them to make still better tools, which in turn had developed their limbs and brains yet further. It was an accelerating, cumulative process; and at its end was Man.

The first true men had tools and weapons only a little better than those of their ancestors a million years earlier, but they could use them with far greater skill. And somewhere in the shadowy centuries that had gone before they had invented the most essential tool of all, though it could be neither seen nor touched. They had learned to speak, and so had won their first great victory over Time. Now the knowledge of one generation could be handed on to the next, so that each age could profit from those that had gone before.

Unlike the animals, who knew only the present, Man had acquired a past; and he was beginning to grope towards a future.

He was also learning to harness the forces of nature; with the taming of fire, he had laid the foundations of technology and left his animal origins far behind. Stone gave way to bronze, and then to iron. Hunting was succeeded by agriculture. The tribe grew into the village, the village into the town. Speech became eternal, thanks to certain marks on stone and clay and papyrus. Presently he invented philosophy, and religion. And he peopled the sky, not altogether inaccurately with gods.

As his body became more and more defenceless, so his means of offence became steadily more frightful. With stone and bronze and iron and steel he had run the gamut of everything that could pierce and slash, and quite early in time he had learned how to strike down his victims from a distance. The spear, the bow, the gun and finally the guided missile had given him weapons of infinite range and all but infinite power.

Without those weapons, often though he had used them against himself, Man would never have conquered his world. Into them he had put his heart and soul, and for ages they had served him well.

But now, as long as they existed, he was living on borrowed time.

II

T.M.A.-1

7

Special Flight

No matter how many times you left Earth, Dr. Heywood
Floyd told himself, the excitement never really palled. He
had been to Mars once, to the Moon three times, and to the
various space-stations more often than he could remember.
Yet as the moment of take-off approached he was conscious
of a rising tension, a feeling of wonder and awe—yes, and of
nervousness—which put him on the same level as any earth-
lubber about the receive his first baptism of space.

The jet that had rushed him here from Washington, after
that midnight briefing with the President, was now dropping
down towards one of the most familiar, yet most exciting,
landscapes in all the world. There lay the first two generations of the Space Age, spanning twenty miles of the
Florida coast. To the south, outlined by winking red warning lights, were the giant gantries of the Saturns and
Neptunes, that had set men on the path to the planets, and
had now passed into history. Near the horizon, a gleaming
silver tower bathed in floodlights, stood the last of the
Saturn V's, for almost twenty years a national monument
and place of pilgrimage. Not far away, looming against the
sky like a man-made mountain, was the incredible bulk of
the Vertical Assembly Building, still the largest single structure on Earth.

But these things now belonged to the past, and he was
flying towards the future. As they banked, Dr. Floyd could
see below him a maze of buildings, then a great airstrip,
then a broad, dead-straight scar across the flat Florida land-

scape—the multiple rails of a giant launching track. At its end, surrounded by vehicles and gantries, a spaceplane lay gleaming in a pool of light, being prepared for its leap to the stars. In a sudden failure of perspective, brought on by his swift changes of speed and height, it seemed to Floyd that he was looking down on a small silver moth, caught in the beam of a flashlight.

Then the tiny, scurrying figures on the ground brought home to him the real size of the spacecraft; it must have been two hundred feet across the narrow 'V' of its wings. And that enormous vehicle, Floyd told himself with some incredulity—yet also with some pride—is waiting for *me*. As far as he knew, it was the first time that an entire mission had been set up to take a single man to the Moon.

Though it was two o'clock in the morning, a group of reporters and cameramen intercepted him on his way to the floodlit Orion III spacecraft. He knew several of them by sight, for as Chairman of the National Council of Astronautics, the news conference was part of his way of life. This was neither the time nor the place for one, and he had nothing to say; but it was important not to offend the gentlemen of the communications media.

'Dr. Floyd? I'm Jim Forster of Associated News. Could you give us a few words about this flight of yours?'

'I'm very sorry—I can't say anything.'

'But you *did* meet with the President earlier this evening?' asked a familiar voice.

'Oh—hello, Mike. I'm afraid you've been dragged out of bed for nothing. Definitely no comment.'

'Can you at least confirm or deny that some kind of epidemic has broken out on the Moon?' a TV reporter asked, managing to jog alongside and keep Floyd properly framed in his miniature TV camera.

'Sorry,' said Floyd, shaking his head.

'What about the quarantine?' asked another reporter. 'How long will it be kept on?'

'Still no comment.'

'Dr. Floyd,' demanded a very short and determined lady of the Press, 'what possible justification can there be for this total blackout of news from the Moon? Has it anything to do with the political situation?'

'*What* political situation?' Floyd asked dryly. There was a sprinkling of laughter, and someone called, 'Have a good trip, Doctor!' as he made his way into the sanctuary of the boarding gantry.

As long as he could remember it had been not a 'situation' so much as a permanent crisis. Since the 1970's the world had been dominated by two problems which, ironically, tended to cancel each other out.

Though birth control was cheap, reliable and endorsed by all the main religions, it had come too late; the population of the world was now six billion—a third of them in the Chinese Empire. Laws had even been passed in some authoritarian societies limiting families to two children, but their enforcement had proved impracticable. As a result, food was short in every country; even the United States had meatless days, and widespread famine was predicted within fifteen years, despite heroic efforts to farm the sea and to develop synthetic foods.

With the need for international co-operation more urgent than ever, there were still as many frontiers as in any earlier age. In a million years the human race had lost few of its aggressive instincts; along symbolic lines visible only to politicians, the thirty-eight nuclear powers watched each other with belligerent anxiety. Between them they possessed sufficient megatonnage to remove the entire surface crust of the planet. Although there had been—miraculously—no use of atomic weapons, this situation could hardly last for ever.

And now, for their own inscrutable reasons, the Chinese were offering to the smallest have-not nations a complete nuclear capability of fifty warheads and delivery systems.

The cost was under $200,000,000, and easy terms could be arranged.

Perhaps they were only trying to shore up their sagging economy by turning obsolete weapons systems into hard cash, as some observers had suggested. Or perhaps they had discovered methods of warfare so advanced that they no longer had need of such toys; there had been talk of radio-hypnosis from satellite transmitters, compulsion viruses, and blackmail by synthetic diseases for which they alone possessed the antidote. These charming ideas were almost certainly propaganda or pure fantasy, but it was not safe to discount any of them. Every time Floyd took off from Earth he wondered if it would still be there when the time came to return.

The trim stewardess greeted him as he entered the cabin. 'Good morning, Dr. Floyd. I'm Miss Simmons—I'd like to welcome you aboard on behalf of Captain Tynes and our co-pilot, First Officer Ballard.'

'Thank you,' said Floyd with a smile, wondering why stewardesses always had to sound like robot tour guides.

'Take-off's in five minutes,' she said, gesturing into the empty, twenty-passenger cabin. 'You can take any seat you want, but Captain Tynes recommends the forward window seat on the left, if you want to watch the docking operations.'

'I'll do that,' he answered, moving toward the preferred seat. The stewardess fussed over him a while and then moved to her cubicle at the rear of the cabin.

Floyd settled down in his seat, adjusted the safety harness around waist and shoulders, and strapped his brief-case to the adjacent seat. A moment later the loudspeaker came on with a soft popping noise. 'Good morning,' said Miss Simmons' voice. 'This is Special Flight 3, Kennedy to Space Station 1.'

She was determined, it seemed, to go through the full routine for her solitary passenger, and Floyd could not resist a smile as she continued inexorably:

'Our transit time will be fifty-five minutes. Maximum acceleration will be two-gee, and we will be weightless for thirty minutes. Please do not leave your seat until the safety sign is lit.'

Floyd looked over his shoulder and called, 'Thank you.' He caught a glimpse of a slightly embarrassed but charming smile.

He leaned back into his seat and relaxed. This trip, he calculated, would cost the tax-payers slightly over a million dollars. If it was not justified he would be out of his job; but he could always go back to the university and to his interrupted studies of planetary formation.

'Auto-countdown procedures all Go,' the Captain's voice said over the speaker with the soothing, sing-song used in RT chat.

'Lift-off in one minute.'

As always, it seemed more like an hour. Floyd became acutely aware of the gigantic forces coiled up around him, waiting to be released. In the fuel tanks of the two space-craft, and in the power-storage system of the launching track, was pent up the energy of a nuclear bomb. And it would all be used to take him a mere two hundred miles from Earth.

There was none of the old-fashioned FIVE-FOUR-THREE-TWO-ONE-ZERO business, so tough on the human nervous system.

'Launching in fifteen seconds. You will be more comfort-able if you start breathing deeply.'

That was good psychology, and good physiology. Floyd felt himself well charged with oxygen, and ready to tackle anything, when the launching track began to sling its thousand-ton payload out over the Atlantic.

It was hard to tell when they lifted from the track and became airborne, but when the roar of the rockets suddenly doubled its fury, and Floyd found himself sinking deeper and deeper into the cushions of his seat, he knew that the first-stage engines had taken over. He wished he could look out of the window, but it was an effort even to turn his head. Yet there was no discomfort; indeed, the pressure of acceleration and the overwhelming thunder of the motors produced an extraordinary euphoria. His ears singing, the blood pounding in his veins, Floyd felt more alive than he had for years. He was young again, he wanted to sing aloud —which was certainly safe, for no one could possibly hear him.

The mood passed swiftly, as he suddenly realised that he was leaving Earth, and everything he had ever loved. Down there were his three children, motherless since his wife had taken that fatal flight to Europe ten years ago. (*Ten* years? Impossible! Yet it was so . . .) Perhaps for their sake, he should have remarried. . . .

He had almost lost sense of time when the pressure and the noise abruptly slackened, and the cabin speaker announced: 'Preparing to separate from lower stage. Here we go.'

There was a slight jolt; and suddenly Floyd recalled a quotation of Leonardo da Vinci's which he had once seen displayed in a N.A.S.A. office:

'The Great Bird will take its flight on the back of the great bird, bringing glory to the nest where it was born.'

Well, the Great Bird was flying now, beyond all the dreams of da Vinci, and its exhausted companion was winging back to Earth. In a ten-thousand-mile arc the empty lower stage would glide down into the atmosphere, trading speed for distance as it homed on Kennedy. In a few hours, serviced and refuelled, it would be ready again to lift another companion towards the shining silence which it could never reach.

Now, thought Floyd, we are on our own, more than half-way to orbit. When the acceleration came on again, as the upper-stage rockets fired, the thrust was much more gentle; indeed, he felt no more than normal gravity. But it would have been impossible to walk, since 'Up' was straight towards the front of the cabin. If he had been foolish enough to leave his seat he would have crashed at once against the rear wall.

This effect was a little disconcerting, for it seemed that the ship was standing on its tail. To Floyd, who was at the very front of the cabin, all the seats appeared to be fixed on a wall dropping vertically beneath him. He was doing his best to ignore this uncomfortable illusion when dawn exploded outside the ship.

In seconds they shot through veils of crimson and pink and gold and blue into the piercing white of day. Though the windows were heavily tinted to reduce the glare, the probing beams of sunlight that now slowly swept across the cabin left Floyd half-blinded for several minutes. He was in space, yet there was no question of being able to see the stars.

He shielded his eyes with his hands and tried to peer through the window beside him. Out there the swept-back wing of the ship was blazing like white-hot metal in the reflected sunlight; there was utter darkness all around it, and that darkness must be full of stars—but it was impossible to see them.

Weight was slowly ebbing; the rockets were being throttled back as the ship eased itself into orbit. The thunder of the engines dropped to a muted roar, then a gentle hiss, then died into silence. If it had not been for the restraining straps Floyd would have floated out of his seat; his stomach felt as if it was going to do so anyway. He hoped that the pills he had been given half an hour and ten thousand miles ago would perform as per specifications. He had been spacesick just once in his career, and that was much too often.

The pilot's voice was firm and confident as it came over the cabin speaker. 'Please observe all Zero-gee regulations. We will be docking at Space Station 1 in forty-five minutes.'

The stewardess came walking up the narrow corridor to

the right of the closely spaced seats. There was a slight buoyancy about her steps, and her feet came away from the floor reluctantly as if entangled in glue. She was keeping to the bright yellow band of Velcro carpeting that ran the full length of the floor—and of the ceiling. The carpet, and the soles of her sandals, were covered with myriads of tiny hooks, so that they clung together like burrs. This trick of walking in free-fall was immensely reassuring to disoriented passengers.

'Would you like some coffee or tea, Dr. Floyd?' she asked cheerfully.

'No thank you,' he smiled. He always felt like a baby when he had to suck at one of those plastic drinking tubes. The stewardess was still hovering anxiously around him as he popped open his brief-case and prepared to remove his papers.

'Dr. Floyd, may I ask you a question?'

'Certainly,' he answered, looking up over his glasses.

'My fiancé is a geologist at Tycho,' said Miss Simmons, measuring her words carefully, 'and I haven't heard from him for over a week.'

'I'm sorry to hear that; maybe he's away from his base, and out of touch.'

She shook her head. 'He always tells me when that's going to happen. And you can imagine how worried I am—with all these rumours. Is it *really* true about an epidemic on the Moon?'

'If it is, there's no cause for alarm. Remember, there was a quarantine back in '98, over that mutated 'flu virus. A lot of people were sick—but no one died. And that's really all I can say,' he concluded firmly.

Miss Simmons smiled pleasantly and straightened up.

'Well, thank you anyway, Doctor. I'm sorry to have bothered you.'

'No bother at all,' he said gallantly, but not very accurately. Then he buried himself in his endless technical reports, in a desperate last-minute assault on the usual back-log.

He would have no time for reading when he got to the Moon.

8

Orbital Rendezvous

Half an hour later the pilot announced: 'We make contact in ten minutes. Please check your seat harness.'

Floyd obeyed, and put away his papers. It was asking for trouble to read during the celestial juggling act which took place during the last three hundred miles; best to close one's eyes and relax while the spacecraft was nudged back and forth with brief bursts of rocket power.

A few minutes later he caught his first glimpse of Space Station 1, only a few miles away. The sunlight glinted and sparkled from the polished metal surfaces of the slowly revolving, three-hundred-yard-diameter disc. Not far away, drifting in the same orbit, was a swept-back Titov-V space-plane, and close to that an almost spherical Aries-IB, the workhorse of space, with the four stubby legs of its lunar-landing shock absorbers jutting from one side.

The Orion III spacecraft was descending from a higher orbit, which brought the Earth into spectacular view behind the Station. From his altitude of two hundred miles Floyd could see much of Africa and the Atlantic Ocean. There was considerable cloud cover, but he could still detect the blue-green outlines of the Gold Coast.

The central axis of the Space Station, with its docking arms extended, was now slowly swimming towards them. Unlike the structure from which it sprang, it was not rotat-

ing—or, rather, it was running in reverse at a rate which
exactly countered the Station's own spin. Thus a visiting
spacecraft could be coupled to it, for the transfer of personnel or cargo, without being whirled disastrously around.

With the softest of thuds, ship and Station made contact.
There were metallic, scratching noises from outside, then
the brief hissing of air as pressures equalised. A few seconds
later the airlock door opened, and a man wearing the light,
close-fitting slacks and short-sleeved shirt which was almost
the uniform of Space Station personnel came into the cabin.

'Pleased to meet you, Dr. Floyd. I'm Nick Miller, Station
Security; I'm to look after you until the shuttle leaves.'

They shook hands, then Floyd smiled at the stewardess
and said: 'Please give my compliments to Captain Tynes,
and thank him for the smooth ride. Perhaps I'll see you on
the way home.'

Very cautiously—it was more than a year since he had last
been weightless and it would be some time before he regained his spacelegs—he hauled himself hand over hand
through the airlock and into the large, circular chamber at
the axis of the Space Station. It was a heavily padded room,
its walls covered with recessed handholds; Floyd gripped
one of these firmly while the whole chamber started to
rotate, until it matched the spin of the Station.

As it gained speed, faint and ghostly gravitational fingers
began to clutch at him, and he drifted slowly towards the
circular wall. Now he was standing, swaying back and forth
gently like seaweed in the surge of the tide, on what had
magically become a curving floor. The centrifugal force of
the Station's spin had taken hold of him; it was very feeble
here, so near the axis, but would increase steadily as he
moved outwards.

From the central transit chamber he followed Miller down
a curving stair. At first his weight was so slight that he had
almost to force himself downwards, by holding on to the
handrail. Not until he reached the passenger lounge, on the

outer skin of the great revolving disc, had he acquired enough weight to move around almost normally.

The lounge had been redecorated since his last visit, and had acquired several new facilities. Besides the usual chairs, small tables, restaurant, and post office there was now a barber's shop, drugstore, movie theatre, and a souvenir shop selling photographs and slides of lunar and planetary landscapes, guaranteed genuine pieces of Luniks, Rangers and Surveyors, all neatly mounted in plastic, and exorbitantly priced.

'Can I get you anything while we're waiting?' Miller asked. 'We board in about thirty minutes.'

'I could do with a cup of black coffee—two lumps—and I'd like to call Earth.'

'Right, Doctor—I'll get the coffee—the phones are over there.'

The picturesque booths were only a few yards from a barrier with two entrances labelled 'WELCOME TO THE U.S. SECTION' and 'WELCOME TO THE SOVIET SECTION'. Beneath these were notices which read, in English, Russian, and Chinese, French, German and Spanish:

'PLEASE HAVE READY YOUR: Passport. Visa. Medical Certificate. Transportation Permit. Weight Declaration.'

There was a rather pleasant symbolism about the fact that as soon as they had passed through the barriers, in either direction, passengers were free to mix again. The division was purely for administrative purposes.

Floyd, after checking that the Area Code for the U.S. was still eighty-one, punched his twelve-digit home number, dropped his plastic all-purpose credit card into the pay slot, and was through in thirty seconds.

Washington was still sleeping, for it was several hours to dawn, but he would not disturb anyone. His housekeeper would get the message from the recorder as soon as she awoke.

'Miss Flemming—this is Dr. Floyd. Sorry I had to leave

in such a hurry. Would you please call my office and ask
them to collect the car—it's at Dulles Airport and the key
is with Mr. Bailey, Senior Flight Control Officer. Next, will
you call the Chevy Chase Country Club and leave a message
for the secretary. I definitely *won't* be able to play in the
tennis tournament next weekend. Give my apologies—I'm
afraid they were counting on me. Then call Downtown
Electronics and tell them that if the video in my study isn't
fixed by—oh, Wednesday—they can take the damn' thing
back.' He paused for breath, and tried to think of any other
crises or problems that might arise during the days ahead.

'If you run short of cash speak to the office; they can get
urgent messages to me, but I may be too busy to answer.
Give my love to the children, and say I'll be back as soon as
I can. Oh hell—here's someone I don't want to see—I'll call
from the Moon if I can—goodbye.'

Floyd tried to duck out of the booth, but it was too late;
he had already been spotted. Bearing down on him through
the Soviet Section exit was Dr. Dimitri Moisewitch, of the
U.S.S.R. Academy of Science.

Dimitri was one of Floyd's best friends, and for that very
reason he was the last person he wished to talk to, here and
now.

9

Moon Shuttle

The Russian astronomer was tall, slender and blond, and
his unlined face belied his fifty-five years—the last ten of
which had been spent building up the giant radio observatory on the far side of the Moon, where two thousand miles
of solid rock would shield it from the electronic racket of
Earth.

'Why, Heywood,' he said, shaking hands firmly. 'It's a small universe. How are you—and your charming children?'

'We're fine,' Floyd replied warmly, but with a slightly distracted air. 'We often talk about the wonderful time you gave us last summer.' He was sorry he could not sound more sincere; they really had enjoyed a week's vacation in Odessa with Dimitri during one of the Russian's visits to Earth.

'And you—I suppose you're on your way up?' Dimitri enquired.

'Er, yes—my flight leaves in half an hour,' answered Floyd. 'Do you know Mr. Miller?'

The Security Officer had now approached, and was standing at a respectful distance holding a plastic cup full of coffee.

'Of course. But *please* put that down, Mr. Miller. This is Dr. Floyd's last chance to have a civilised drink—let's not waste it. No—I insist.'

They followed Dimitri out of the main lounge into the observation section, and soon were sitting at a table under a dim light watching the moving panorama of the stars. Space Station 1 revolved once a minute, and the centrifugal force generated by this slow spin produced an artificial gravity equal to the Moon's. This, it had been discovered, was a good compromise between Earth gravity and no gravity at all; moreover, it gave Moon-bound passengers a chance to become acclimatised.

Outside the almost invisible windows, Earth and stars marched in a silent procession. At the moment this side of the Station was tilted away from the Sun; otherwise it would have been impossible to look out, for the lounge would have been blasted with light. Even as it was, the glare of the Earth, filling half the sky, drowned all but the brighter stars.

But Earth was waning, as the Station orbited towards the night side of the planet; in a few minutes it would be a huge black disc, spangled with the lights of cities. And then the sky would belong to the stars.

'Now,' said Dimitri, after he had swiftly downed his first drink, and was toying with the second, 'what's all this about an epidemic in the U.S. Sector? I wanted to go there on this trip. "No, Professor," they told me. "We're very sorry, but there's a strict quarantine until further notice." I pulled all the strings I could; it was no use. Now *you* tell me what's happening.'

Floyd groaned inwardly. Here we go again, he thought. The sooner I'm on that shuttle, headed for the Moon, the happier I'll be.

'The—ah—quarantine is purely a safety precaution,' he said cautiously. 'We're not even sure it's really necessary, but we don't believe in taking chances.'

'But what *is* the disease—what are the symptoms? Could it be extraterrestrial? Do you want any help from our medical services?'

'I'm sorry, Dimitri—we've been asked not to say *anything* at the moment. Thanks for the offer, but we can handle the situation.'

'Hmm,' said Moisewitch, obviously quite unconvinced. 'Seems odd to me that *you*, an astronomer, should be sent up to the Moon to look into an epidemic.'

'I'm only an ex-astronomer; it's years since I did any real research. Now I'm a scientific expert; that means I know nothing about absolutely *everything*.'

'Then do you know what T.M.A.-1 means?'

Miller seemed about to choke on his drink, but Floyd was made of sterner stuff. He looked his old friend straight in the eye, and said calmly: 'T.M.A.-1? What an odd expression. Where did you hear it?'

'Never mind,' retorted the Russian. 'You can't fool me. But if you've run into something you can't handle I hope you don't leave it until too late before you yell for help.'

Miller looked meaningfully at his watch.

'Due to board in five minutes, Dr. Floyd,' he said. 'I think we'd better get moving.'

Though he knew that they still had a good twenty minutes, Floyd got up with haste. Too much haste, for he had forgotten the one-sixth of a gravity. He grabbed the table just in time to prevent a take-off.

'It was fine meeting you, Dimitri,' he said, not quite accurately. 'Hope you have a good trip down to Earth—I'll give you a call as soon as I'm back.'

As they left the lounge, and checked through the U.S. transit barrier, Floyd remarked: 'Phew—that was close. Thanks for rescuing me.'

'You know, Doctor,' said the Security Officer, 'I hope he isn't right.'

'Right about what?'

'About us running into something we can't handle.'

'*That*,' Floyd answered with determination, 'is what I intend to find out.'

Forty-five minutes later the Aries–1B lunar carrier pulled away from the station. There was none of the power and fury of a take-off from Earth—only an almost inaudble, far-off whistling as the low-thrust plasma jets blasted their electrified streams into space. The gentle push lasted for more than fifteen minutes, and the mild acceleration would not have prevented anyone from moving around the cabin. But when it was over, the ship was no longer bound to Earth, as it had been while it still accompanied the Station. It had broken the bonds of gravity and was now a free and independent planet, circling the Sun in an orbit of its own.

The cabin Floyd now had all to himself had been designed for thirty passengers. It was strange, and rather lonely, to see all the empty seats around him, and to have the un-divided attention of the steward and stewardess—not to mention pilot, co-pilot, and two engineers. He doubted that any man in history had ever received such exclusive service, and it was most unlikely that anyone would do so in the future. He recalled the cynical remark of one of the less

reputable pontiffs: 'Now that we have the Papacy, let us
enjoy it.' Well, he would enjoy this trip, and the euphoria
of weightlessness. With the loss of gravity he had—at least
for a while—shed most of his cares. Someone had once said
that you could be terrified in space, but you could not be
worried there. It was perfectly true.

The stewards, it appeared, were determined to make him
eat for the whole twenty-five hours of the trip, and he was
continually fending off unwanted meals. Eating in zero
gravity was no real problem, contrary to the dark forebod-
ings of the early astronauts. He sat at an ordinary table, to
which the plates were clipped, as aboard ship in a rough sea.
All the courses had some element of stickiness, so that they
would not take off and go wandering around the cabin.
Thus a chop would be glued to the plate by a thick sauce,
and a salad kept under control by an adhesive dressing.
With a little skill and care there were few items that could
not be tackled safely; the only things banned were hot
soups and excessively crumbly pastries. Drinks, of course,
were a different matter; all liquids simply had to be kept in
plastic squeeze-tubes.

A whole generation of research by heroic but unsung
volunteers had gone into the design of the washroom, and it
was now considered to be more or less fool-proof. Floyd
investigated it soon after free-fall had begun. He found
himself in a little cubicle with all the fittings of an ordinary
airline toilet, but illuminated with a red light that was very
harsh and unpleasant to the eye. A notice printed in prominent letters announced: 'MOST IMPORTANT! FOR YOUR OWN
COMFORT, PLEASE READ THESE INSTRUCTIONS CAREFULLY!!!'

Floyd sat down (one still tended to do so, even when
weightless) and read the notice several times. When he was
sure there had been no modifications since his last trip, he
pressed the START button.

Close at hand an electric motor began to whirr, and Floyd
felt himself moving. As the notice advised him to do, he

closed his eyes and waited. After a minute a bell chimed softly and he looked around.

The light had now changed to a soothing pinkish white; but, more important, he was under gravity again. Only the faintest vibration revealed that it was a spurious gravity, caused by the carousel-like spin of the whole toilet compartment. Floyd picked up a piece of soap, and watched it drop in slow motion; he judged that the centrifugal force was about a quarter of a normal gravity. But that was quite enough; it would ensure that everything moved in the right direction, in the one place where this mattered most.

He pressed the STOP FOR EXIT button, and closed his eyes again. Weight slowly ebbed as the rotation ceased, the bell gave a double chime, and the red warning light was back. The door was then locked in the right position to let him glide out into the cabin, where he adhered as quickly as possible to the carpet. He had long ago exhausted the novelty of weightlessness, and was grateful for the Velcro slippers that allowed him to walk almost normally.

There was plenty to occupy his time, even if he did nothing but sit and read. When he tired of official reports and memoranda and minutes he would plug his foolscap-sized newspad into the ship's information circuit and scan the latest reports from Earth. One by one he would conjure up the world's major electronic papers; he knew the codes of the more important ones by heart, and had no need to consult the list on the back of his pad. Switching to the display unit's short-term memory, he would hold the front page while he quickly searched the headlines and noted the items that interested him. Each had its own two-digit reference; when he punched that, the postage-stamp-sized rectangle would expand until it neatly filled the screen, and he could read it with comfort. When he had finished he would flash back to the complete page and select a new subject for detailed examination.

Floyd sometimes wondered if the Newspad, and the fan-

tastic technology behind it, was the last word in man's quest
for perfect communications. Here he was, far out in space,
speeding away from Earth at thousands of miles an hour,
yet in a few milliseconds he could see the headlines of any
newspaper he pleased. (That very word 'newspaper', of
course, was an anachronistic hang-over into the age of
electronics.) The text was updated automatically on every
hour; even if one read only the English versions one could
spend an entire lifetime doing nothing but absorb the ever-
changing flow of information from the news satellites.

It was hard to imagine how the system could be improved
or made more convenient. But sooner or later, Floyd
guessed, it would pass away, to be replaced by something as
unimaginable as the Newspad itself would have been to
Caxton or Gutenberg.

There was another thought which a scanning of those tiny
electronic headlines often invoked. The more wonderful the
means of communication, the more trivial, tawdry or de-
pressing its contents seemed to be. Accidents, crimes, natural
and man-made disasters, threats of conflict, gloomy edi-
torials—these still seemed to be the main concern of the
millions of words being sprayed into the ether. Yet Floyd
also wondered if this was altogether a bad thing; the news-
papers of Utopia, he had long ago decided, would be terribly
dull.

From time to time the captain and the other members of
the crew came into the cabin and exchanged a few words
with him. They treated their distinguished passenger with
awe, and were doubtless burning with curiosity about his
mission, but were too polite to ask any questions or even to
drop any hints.

Only the charming little stewardess seemed completely at
ease in his presence. As Floyd quickly discovered, she came
from Bali, and had carried beyond the atmosphere some of
the grace and mystery of that still largely unspoilt island.
One of his strangest, and most enchanting, memories of the

entire trip was her zero-gravity demonstration of some classical Balinese dance movements, with the lovely, blue-green crescent of the waning Earth as a backdrop.

There was one sleep period, when the main cabin lights were switched off and Floyd fastened down his arms and legs with the elastic sheets that would prevent him from drifting away into space. It seemed a crude arrangement— but here in zero-gravity his unpadded couch was more comfortable than the most luxurious mattress on Earth.

When he had strapped himself in, Floyd dozed off quickly enough, but woke up once in a drowsy, half-conscious condition, to be completely baffled by his strange surroundings. For a moment he thought that he was in the middle of some dimly lit Chinese lantern; the faint glow from the other cubicles around him gave that impression. Then he said to himself, firmly and successfully: 'Go to sleep, boy. This is just an ordinary moon-shuttle.'

When he awoke, the Moon had swallowed up half the sky, and the braking manœuvres were about to begin. The wide arc of windows set in the curving wall of the passenger section now looked out on to the open sky, not the approaching globe, so he moved into the control cabin. Here, on the rear-view TV screens, he could watch the final stages of the descent.

The approaching lunar mountains were utterly unlike those of Earth; they lacked the dazzling caps of snow, the green, close-fitting garments of vegetation, the moving crowns of cloud. Nevertheless, the fierce contrasts of light and shadow gave them a strange beauty of their own. The laws of earthly aesthetics did not apply here; this world had been shaped and moulded by other than terrestrial forces, operating over aeons of time unknown to the young, verdant Earth, with its fleeting Ice Ages, its swiftly rising and falling seas, its mountain ranges dissolving like mists before the dawn. Here was age inconceivable—but not death, for the Moon had never lived—until now.

The descending ship was poised almost above the line dividing night from day, and directly below was a chaos of jagged shadows and brilliant, isolated peaks catching the first light of the slow lunar dawn. That would be a fearful place to attempt a landing, even with all possible electronic aids; but they were slowly drifting away from it, towards the night side of the Moon.

Then Floyd saw, as his eyes grew more accustomed to the fainter illumination, that the night land was not wholly dark. It was aglow with a ghostly light, in which peaks and valleys and plains could be clearly seen. The Earth, a giant moon to the Moon, was flooding the land below with its radiance.

On the pilot's panel, lights flashed above radar screens, numbers came and went on computer displays, clocking off the distance of the approaching Moon. They were still more than a thousand miles away when weight returned as the jets began their gentle but steady deceleration. For ages, it seemed, the Moon slowly expanded across the sky, the Sun sank below the horizon, and at last a single giant crater filled the field of view. The shuttle was falling towards its central peaks—and suddenly Floyd noticed that near one of those peaks a brilliant light was flashing with a regular rhythm. It might have been an airport beacon back on Earth, and he started at it with a tightening of the throat. It was proof that men had established another foothold on the Moon.

Now the crater had expanded so much that its ramparts were slipping below the horizon, and the smaller craterlets that peppered its interior were beginning to disclose their real size. Some of these, tiny though they had seemed from far out in space, were miles across, and could have swallowed whole cities.

Under its automatic controls the shuttle was sliding down the starlit sky, towards that barren landscape glimmering in the light of the great gibbous Earth. Now a voice was calling somewhere above the whistle of the jets and the electronic beepings that came and went through the cabin.

'Clavius Control to Special 14, you are coming in nicely. Please make manual check of landing gear lock, hydraulic pressure, shock pad inflation.'

The pilot pressed sundry switches, green lights flashed, and he called back, 'All manual checks completed. Landing gear lock, hydraulic pressure, shock pad O.K.'

'Confirmed,' said the Moon, and the descent continued wordlessly. Though there was still plenty of talking, it was all being done by machines, flashing binary impulses to one another at a thousand times the rate their slow-thinking makers could communicate.

Some of the mountain peaks were already towering above the shuttle; now the ground was only a few thousand feet away, and the beacon light was a brilliant star, flashing steadily above a group of low buildings and odd vehicles. In the final stage of the descent the jets seemed to be playing some strange tune; they pulsed on and off, making the last fine adjustments to the thrust.

Abruptly, a swirling cloud of dust hid everything, the jets gave one final spurt, and the shuttle rocked very slightly, like a rowboat when a small wave goes by. It was some minutes before Floyd could really accept the silence that now enfolded him and the weak gravity that gripped his limbs.

He had made, utterly without incident and in little more than one day, the incredible journey of which men had dreamed for two thousand years. After a normal, routine flight, he had landed on the Moon.

10

Clavius Base

Clavius, a hundred-and-fifty miles in diameter, is the second largest crater on the visible face of the Moon, and lies in the centre of the Southern Highlands. It is very old; ages of vulcanism and bombardment from space have scarred its walls and pock-marked its floor. But since the last era of crater-formation, when the debris from the asteroid belt was still battering the inner planets, it had known peace for half a billion years.

Now there were new, strange stirrings on and below its surface, for here Man was establishing his first permanent bridgehead on the Moon. Clavius Base could, in an emergency, be entirely self-supporting. All the necessities of life were produced from the local rocks, after they had been crushed, heated, and chemically processed. Hydrogen, oxygen, carbon, nitrogen, phosphorous—all these, and most of the other elements, could be found inside the Moon, if anyone knew where to look for them.

The Base was a closed system, like a tiny working model of Earth itself, recycling all the chemicals of life. The atmosphere was purified in a vast 'hothouse'—a large, circular room buried just below the lunar surface. Under blazing lamps by night, and filtered sunlight by day, acres of stubby green plants grew in warm, moist atmosphere. They were special mutations, designed for the express purpose of replenishing the air with oxygen, and providing food as a by-product.

More food was produced by chemical processing systems and algae culture. Although the green scum circulating through yards of transparent plastic tubes would have scarcely appealed to a gourmet, the biochemists could con-

vert it into chops and steaks only an expert could distinguish
from the real thing.

The eleven hundred men and six hundred women who
made up the personnel of the Base were all highly trained
scientists and technicians, carefully selected before they had
left Earth. Though lunar living was now virtually free from
the hardships, disadvantages and occasional dangers of the
early days, it was still psychologically demanding, and not
recommended for anyone suffering from claustrophobia.
Since it was expensive and time-consuming to cut a large
underground base out of solid rock or compacted lava, the
standard one-man 'living module' was a room only about
six feet wide, ten feet long, and eight feet high.

Each room was attractively furnished and looked very
much like a good motel suite, with convertible sofa, TV,
small Hi-Fi set, and vision phone. Moreover, by a simple
trick of interior decoration, the one unbroken wall could be
converted by the flip of a switch into a convincing terrestrial
landscape. There was a choice of eight views.

This touch of luxury was typical of the Base, though it
was sometimes hard to explain its necessity to the folk back
on Earth. Every man and women in Clavius had cost a
hundred thousand dollars in training and transport and
housing; it was worth a little extra to maintain their peace
of mind. This was not art for art's sake, but art for the sake
of sanity.

One of the attractions of life in the Base—and on the
Moon as a whole—was undoubtedly the low gravity, which
produced a sense of general well-being. However, this had
its dangers, and it was several weeks before an emigrant
from Earth could adapt to it. On the Moon the human body
had to learn a whole new set of reflexes. It had, for the first
time, to distinguish between mass and weight.

A man who weighed one hundred and eighty pounds on
Earth might be delighted to discover that he weighed only
thirty pounds on the Moon. As long as he moved in a

straight line at a uniform speed he felt a wonderful sense of
buoyancy. But as soon as he attempted to change course, to
turn corners, or to stop suddenly—*then* he would find that his
full one hundred and eighty pounds of mass, or inertia, was
still there. For that was fixed and unalterable—the same on
Earth, Moon, Sun or in free space. Before one could be
properly adapted to lunar living, therefore, it was essential
to learn that all objects were now six times as sluggish as
their mere weight would suggest. It was a lesson usually
driven home by numerous collisions and hard knocks, and
old lunar hands kept their distance from newcomers until
they were acclimatised.

With its complex of workshops, offices, store-rooms,
computer centre, generators, garage, kitchen, laboratories,
and food processing plant, Clavius Base was a miniature
world in itself. And, ironically, many of the skills that had
been used to build this underground empire had been developed during the half-century of the Cold War.

Any man who had ever worked in a hardened missile site
would have felt at home in Clavius. Here on the Moon
were the same arts and hardware of underground living,
and of protection against a hostile environment; but here
they had turned to the purposes of peace. After ten thousand
years man had at last found something as exciting as
war. Unfortunately, not all nations had yet realised that
fact.

.   .   .   .   .

The mountains that had been so prominent just before
landing had mysteriously disappeared, hidden from sight
below the steeply curving lunar horizon. Around the spacecraft was a flat, grey plain, brilliantly lit by the slanting
earthlight. Although the sky was, of course, completely
black, only the brighter stars and planets could be seen,
unless the eyes were shaded from the surface glare.

Several very odd vehicles were rolling up to the Aries-1B spaceship—cranes, hoists, servicing trucks—some automatic, some operated by a driver in a small pressure cabin. Most of them moved on balloon tyres, for this smooth, level plain posed no transportation difficulties; but one tanker rolled on the peculiar flex-wheels which had proved one of the best all-purpose ways of getting around on the Moon. A series of flat plates arranged in a circle, each plate independently mounted and sprung, the flex-wheel had many of the advantages of the caterpillar track from which it had evolved. It would adapt its shape and diameter to the terrain over which it was moving, and, unlike a caterpillar track, would continue to function even if a few sections were missing.

A small bus with an extension tube like a stubby elephant trunk was now nuzzling affectionately up against the spacecraft. A few seconds later there were bangings and bumpings from outside, followed by the sound of hissing air as connections were made and pressure was equalised. The inner door of the airlock opened, and the welcoming delegation entered.

It was led by Ralph Halvorsen, the Administrator of the Southern Province—which meant not only the Base but also any exploring parties that operated from it. With him was his Chief Scientist, Dr. Roy Michaels, a grizzled little geophysicist whom Floyd knew from previous visits, and half a dozen senior scientists and executives. They greeted him with respectful relief; from the Administrator downwards, it was obvious that they looked forward to a chance of unloading some of their worries.

'Very pleased to have you with us, Dr. Floyd,' said Halvorsen. 'Did you have a good trip?'

'Excellent,' Floyd answered. 'It couldn't have been better. The crew looked after me very well.'

He exchanged the usual small-talk that courtesy demanded while the bus rolled away from the spacecraft; by unspoken agreement, no one mentioned the reason for his visit. After travelling a thousand feet from the landing site the bus came to a large sign which read:

WELCOME TO CLAVIUS BASE
U.S. Astronautical Engineering Corps
1994

It then dived into a cutting which took it quickly below ground level. A massive door opened ahead, then closed behind them. This happened again, and yet a third time. When the last door had closed there was a great roaring of air, and they were back in atmosphere once more, in the shirt-sleeve environment of the Base.

After a short walk through a tunnel packed with pipes and cables, and echoing hollowly with rhythmic thumpings and throbbings, they arrived in executive territory, and Floyd found himself back in the familiar environment of type-writers, office computers, girl assistants, wall charts and ringing telephones. As they paused outside the door labelled 'ADMINISTRATOR', Halvorsen said diplomatically: 'Dr. Floyd and I will be along to the briefing room in a couple of minutes.'

The others nodded, made agreeable sounds, and drifted off down the corridor. But before Halvorsen could usher Floyd into his office there was an interruption. The door opened, and a small figure hurled itself at the Administrator.

'Daddy! You've been Topside! and you *promised* to take me!'

'Now, Diana,' said Halvorsen, with exasperated tender-ness, 'I only said I'd take you if I could. But I've been very busy meeting Dr. Floyd. Shake hands with him—he's just come from Earth.'

The little girl—Floyd judged that she was about eight—extended a limp hand. Her face was vaguely familiar, and Floyd became aware that the Administrator was looking at him with a quizzical smile. With a shock of recollection he understood why.

'I don't believe it!' he exclaimed. 'When I was here last, she was just a baby!'

'She had her fourth birthday last week,' Halvorsen answered proudly. 'Children grow fast in this low gravity. But they don't age so quickly—they'll live longer than we do.'

Floyd stared in fascination at the self-assured little lady, noting the graceful carriage and the unusually delicate bone-structure. 'It's nice to meet you again, Diana,' he said. Then something—perhaps sheer curiosity, perhaps politeness—impelled him to add: 'Would *you* like to go to Earth?'

Her eyes widened with astonishment; then she shook her head.

'It's a nasty place; you hurt yourself when you fall down. Besides, there are too many people.'

So here, Floyd told himself, is the first generation of the Spaceborn; there would be more of them in years to come. Though there was sadness in this thought, there was also a great hope. When Earth was tamed and tranquil, and perhaps a little tired, there would still be scope for those who loved freedom, for the tough pioneers, the restless adventurers. But their tools would not be axe and gun and canoe and wagon; they would be nuclear power plant and plasma drive and hydroponic farm. The time was fast approaching when Earth, like all mothers, must say farewell to her children.

With a mixture of threats and promises, Halvorsen managed to evict his determined offspring, and led Floyd into the office. The Administrator's suite was only about fifteen feet square, but it managed to contain all the fittings and status symbols of the typical $50,000-a-year head of a department. Signed photographs of important politicians—including the President of the United States and the

Secretary General of the United Nations—adorned one wall, while signed photos of celebrated astronauts covered most of another.

Floyd sank into a comfortable leather chair and was given a glass of 'sherry', courtesy of the Lunar biochemical labs. 'How's it going, Ralph?' Floyd asked, sipping the drink with caution, then with approval.

'Not too bad,' Halvorsen replied. 'However, there *is* something you'd better know about, before you go in there.'

'What is it?'

'Well, I suppose you could describe it as a morale problem,' Halvorsen sighed.

'Oh?'

'It isn't serious yet, but it's getting there fast.'

'The news blackout,' Floyd said flatly.

'Right,' Halvorsen replied. 'My people are getting very steamed up about it. After all, most of them have families back on Earth; they probably believe they're all dead of moon-plague.'

'I'm sorry about that,' said Floyd, 'but no one could think of a better cover story, and so far it's worked. By the way—I met Moisewitch at the Space Station, and even *he* bought it.'

'Well, that should make Security happy.'

'Not too happy—he'd heard of T.M.A.-1; rumours are beginning to leak out. But we just can't issue any statement, until we know what the damn thing is and whether our Chinese friends are behind it.'

'Dr. Michaels thinks he has the answer to that. He's dying to tell you.'

Floyd drained his glass.

'And I'm dying to hear him. Let's go.'

11

Anomaly

The briefing took place in a large rectangular chamber that could hold a hundred people with ease. It was equipped with the latest optical and electronic displays and would have looked like a model conference room but for the numerous posters, pin-ups, notices and amateur paintings, which indicated that it was also the centre of the local cultural life. Floyd was particularly struck by a collection of signs, obviously assembled with loving care, which carried such messages as 'PLEASE KEEP OFF THE GRASS', 'NO PARKING ON EVEN DAYS', 'DEFENSE DE FUMER', 'TO THE BEACH', 'CATTLE CROSSING', 'SOFT SHOULDERS' and 'DO NOT FEED THE ANIMALS'. If these were genuine—as they certainly appeared to be —their transportation from Earth had cost a small fortune. There was a touching defiance about them; on this hostile world men could still joke about the things they had been forced to leave behind—and which their children would never miss.

A crowd of forty of fifty people was waiting for Floyd, and everyone rose politely as he entered behind the Administrator. As he nodded at several familiar faces, Floyd whispered to Halvorsen: 'I'd like to say a few words before the briefing.'

Floyd sat down in the front row, while the Administrator ascended the rostrum and looked round his audience.

'Ladies and gentlemen,' Halvorsen began, 'I needn't tell you that this is a very important occasion. We are delighted to have Dr. Heywood Floyd with us. We all know him by reputation, and many of us are acquainted with him personally. He has just completed a special flight from Earth to be here, and before the briefing he has a few words for us. Dr. Floyd.'

Floyd walked to the rostrum amid a sprinkling of polite applause, surveyed the audience with a smile, and said: 'Thank you—I only want to say this. The President has asked me to convey his appreciation of your outstanding work, which we hope the world will soon be able to recognise. I'm quite aware,' he continued carefully, 'that some of you —perhaps most of you—are anxious that the present veil of secrecy be withdrawn; you would not be scientists if you thought otherwise.'

He caught a glimpse of Dr. Michaels, whose face was creased in a slight frown which brought out a long scar down his right cheek—presumably the aftermath of some accident in space. The geologist, he was well aware, had been protesting vigorously against what he called this 'cops and robbers nonsense'.

'But I would remind you,' Floyd continued, 'that this is a quite extraordinary situation. We must be absolutely sure of our own facts; if we make errors now there may be no second chance—so please be patient a little longer. Those are also the wishes of the President.

'That's all I have to say. Now I'm ready for your report.'

He walked back to his seat; the Administrator said, 'Thank you very much, Dr. Floyd,' and nodded, rather brusquely, to his Chief Scientist. On cue, Dr. Michaels walked up to the rostrum, and the lights faded out.

A photograph of the Moon flashed on to the screen. At the very centre of the disc was a brilliant white crater ring, from which a striking pattern of rays fanned out. It looked exactly as if someone had hurled a bag of flour at the face of the Moon, and it had spattered out in all directions.

'On this vertical photograph,' said Michaels, pointing to the central crater, 'Tycho is even more conspicuous than when seen from Earth; then it's rather near the edge of the Moon. But observed from *this* viewpoint—looking straight down from a thousand miles up—you'll see how it dominates the entire hemisphere.'

He let Floyd absorb this unfamiliar view of a familiar object, then continued: 'During the past year we have been conducting a magnetic survey of the region, from a low-level satellite. It was completed only last month—and this is the result—the map that started all the trouble.'

Another picture flashed on the screen; it looked like a contour map, though it showed magnetic intensity, not height above sea level. For the most part, the lines were roughly parallel and spaced well apart; but in one corner of the map they became suddenly packed together, to form a series of concentric circles—like a drawing of a knot-hole in a piece of wood.

Even to an untrained eye it was obvious that something peculiar had happened to the Moon's magnetic field in this region; and in large letters across the bottom of the map were the words: 'TYCHO MAGNETIC ANOMALY—ONE (T.M.A.-I).' Stamped on the top right was 'CLASSIFIED'.

'At first we thought it might be an outcrop of magnetic rock, but all the geological evidence was against it. And not even a big nickel-iron meteorite could produce a field as intense as this; so we decided to have a look.

'The first party discovered nothing—just the usual level terrain, buried beneath a very thin layer of moondust. They sank a drill in the exact centre of the magnetic field, to get a core sample for study. Twenty feet down, the drill stopped. So the survey party started to dig—not an easy job in spacesuits, I can assure you.

'What they found brought them back to Base in a hurry. We sent out a bigger team, with better equipment. They excavated for two weeks—with the result you know.'

The darkened assembly room became suddenly hushed and expectant as the picture on the screen changed. Though everyone had seen it many times, there was not a person who failed to crane forward as if hoping to find new details. On Earth and Moon less than a hundred people had so far been allowed to set eyes on this photograph.

It showed a man in a bright red and yellow spacesuit, standing at the bottom of an excavation, and supporting a surveyor's rod marked off in tenths of a metre. It was obviously a night shot, and might have been taken anywhere on the Moon or Mars. But until now no planet had ever produced a scene like this.

The object before which the spacesuited man was posing was a vertical slab of jet-black material, about ten feet high and five feet wide; it reminded Floyd, somewhat ominously of a giant tombstone. Perfectly-sharp-edged and symetrical, it was so black it seemed to have swallowed up the light falling upon it; there was no surface detail at all. It was impossible to tell whether it was made of stone, or metal, or plastic—or some material altogether unknown to man.

'T.M.A.-1,' Dr. Michaels declared, almost reverently. 'It looks brand new, doesn't it? I can hardly blame those who thought it was just a few years old, and tried to connect it with the third Chinese Expedition, back in '98. But I never belived that—and now we've been able to date it positively, from local geological evidence.

'My colleagues and I, Dr. Floyd, will stake our reputations on this. T.M.A.-1 has nothing to do with the Chinese. Indeed, it has nothing to do with the human race—for when it was buried, there *were* no humans.

'You see, it is approximately three million years old. What you are now looking at is the first evidence of intelligent life beyond the Earth.'

12

Journey by Earthlight

MACRO-CRATER PROVINCE: Extends S. from near center of the visible face of moon, E. of Central Crater Province. Densely pocked with impact craters; many large, and including the largest on moon; in N. some craters fractured from impact forming Mare Imbrium. Rough surfaces almost everywhere, except for some crater bottoms. Most surfaces in slopes, mostly 10° to 12°; some crater bottoms nearly level.

LANDING AND MOVEMENT: Landing generally difficult because of rough, sloping surfaces; less difficult in some level crater bottoms. Movement possible almost everywhere but route selection required; less difficult on some level crater bottoms.

CONSTRUCTION: Generally moderately difficult because of slope, and numerous large blocks in loose material; excavation of lava difficult in some crater bottoms.

Tycho. Post-Maria crater, 54 miles diameter, rim 7,900 feet above surroundings; bottom 12,000 feet deep; has the most prominent ray system on the moon, some rays extending more than 500 miles.

(Extract from *Engineer Special Study of the Surface of the Moon*, Office, Chief of Engineers, Department of the Army. U.S. Geological Survey, Washington, 1961.)

.   .   .   .   .

The mobile lab now rolling across the crater plain at fifty miles an hour looked rather like an outsized trailer mounted on eight flex-wheels. But it was very much more than this; it was a self-contained base in which twenty men could live and work for several weeks. Indeed, it was virtually a landgoing spaceship—and in an emergency it could even fly.

If it came to a crevasse or canyon which was too large to detour, and too steep to enter, it could hop across the obstacle on its four underjets.

As he peered out of the window, Floyd could see stretching ahead of him a well-defined trail, where dozens of vehicles had left a hard-packed band in the friable surface of the Moon. At regular intervals along the track were tall, slender rods, each carrying a flashing light. No one could possibly get lost, on the two-hundred-mile journey from Clavius Base to T.M.A.-1, even though it was still night and the Sun would not rise for several hours.

The stars overhead were only a little brighter, or more numerous, than on a clear night from the high plateaus of New Mexico or Colorado. But there were two things in that coal-black sky that destroyed any illusion of Earth.

The first was Earth itself—a blazing beacon hanging above the northern horizon. The light pouring down from that giant half-globe was dozens of times more brilliant than the full moon, and it covered all this land with a cold, blue-green phosphorescence.

The second celestial apparition was a faint, pearly cone of light slanting up the eastern sky. It became brighter and brighter towards the horizon, hinting of great fires just concealed below the edge of the Moon. Here was a pale glory that no man had ever seen from Earth, save during the few moments of a total eclipse. It was the corona, harbinger of the lunar dawn, giving notice that before long the Sun would smite this sleeping land.

As he sat with Halvorsen and Michaels in the forward observation lounge, immediately beneath the driver's position, Floyd found his thoughts turning again and again to the three-million-year-wide gulf that had just opened up before him. Like all scientifically literate men, he was used to considering far longer periods of time—but they had concerned only the movements of stars and the slow cycles of the inanimate universe. Mind or intelligence had not been involved; those aeons were empty of all that touched the emotions.

Three million years! The infinitely crowded panorama of written history, with its empires and its kings, its triumphs and its tragedies, covered barely one thousandth of this appalling span of time. Not only Man himself, but most of the animals now alive on Earth, did not even exist when this black enigma was so carefully buried here, in the most brilliant and most spectacular of all the craters of the Moon.

That it had been buried, and quite deliberately, Dr. Michaels was absolutely sure. 'At first,' he explained, 'I rather hoped it might mark the site of some underground structure, but our latest excavations have eliminated that. It's sitting on a wide platform of the same black material, with undisturbed rock beneath it. The—*creatures*—who designed it wanted to make sure it stayed put, barring major moonquakes. They were building for eternity.'

There was triumph, and yet sadness, in Michaels' voice, and Floyd could share both emotions. At last, one of man's oldest questions has been answered; here was the proof, beyond all shadow of doubt, that his was not the only intelligence that the universe had brought forth. But with that knowledge, there came again an aching awareness of the immensity of Time. Whatever had passed this way had missed mankind by a hundred thousand generations. Perhaps, Floyd told himself, it was just as well. And yet—what we might have learned from creatures who could cross space, while our ancestors were still living in trees!

A few hundred yards ahead, a signpost was coming up over the Moon's strangely close horizon. At its base was a tent-shaped structure covered with shining silver foil, obviously for protection against the fierce heat of day. As the bus rolled by, Floyd was able to read in the brilliant earthlight:

EMERGENCY DEPOT NO. 3
   20 Kilos Lox
   10 Kilos Water
   20 Foodpaks Mk. 4
   1 Toolkit Type B
   1 Suit Repair Outfit
   ! TELEPHONE !

'Have you thought of *that*?' asked Floyd, pointing out
of the window. 'Suppose the thing's a supply cache, left
behind by an expedition that never returned?'

'It's a possibility,' admitted Michaels. 'That magnetic
field certainly labelled its position, so that it could be easily
found. But it's rather small—it couldn't hold much in the
way of supplies.'

'Why not?' interjected Halvorsen. 'Who knows how big
they were? Perhaps they were only six inches tall, which
would make the thing twenty or thirty storeys high.'

Michaels shook his head.

'Out of the question,' he protested. 'You can't have very
small, intelligent creatures; you need a minimum brain size.'

Michaels and Halvorsen, Floyd had noticed, usually took
opposing viewpoints, yet there appeared to be little personal
hostility or friction between them. They seemed to respect
each other, and simply agreed to disagree.

There was certainly little agreement anywhere about the
nature of T.M.A.-1—or the Tycho Monolith, as some preferred to call it, retaining part of the abbreviation. In the
six hours since he had landed on the Moon, Floyd had
heard a dozen theories, but had committed himself to none.
Shrine, survey marker, tomb, geophysical instrument—
these were perhaps the favourite suggestions, and some of
the protagonists grew very heated in their defence. A good
many bets had already been placed, and a lot of money
would change hands when the truth was finally known—if,
indeed, it ever was.

So far, the hard black material of the slab had resisted all the rather mild attempts that Michaels and his colleagues had made to obtain samples. They had no doubt that a laser beam would cut into it—for surely, nothing could resist *that* frightful concentration of energy—but the decision to employ such violent measures would be left to Floyd. He had already decided that X-rays, sonic probes, neutron beams and all other non-destructive means of investigation would be brought into play before he called up the heavy artillery of the laser. It was the mark of a barbarian to destroy something one could not understand; but perhaps men were barbarians, besides the creatures who had made this thing.

And where *could* they have come from? The Moon itself? No, that was utterly impossible. If there had ever been indigenous life on this barren world, it had been destroyed during the last crater-forming epoch, when most of the lunar surface was white-hot.

Earth? Very unlikely, though perhaps not quite impossible. Any advanced terrestrial civilisation—presumably a non-human one—back in the Pleistocene Era would have left many other traces of its existence. We would have known all about it, thought Floyd, long before we got to the Moon.

That left two alternatives—the planets, and the stars. Yet all the evidence was against intelligent life elsewhere in the Solar System—or indeed life of *any* kind except on Earth and Mars. The inner planets were too hot, the outer ones far too cold, unless one descended into their atmosphere to depths where the pressures amounted to hundreds of tons to the square inch.

So perhaps these visitors had come from the stars—yet that was even more incredible. As he looked up at the constellations strewn across the ebon lunar sky, Floyd remembered how often his fellow scientists had 'proved' that interstellar travel was impossible. The journey from Earth to Moon was still fairly impressive, but the very nearest star was a hundred million times more distant. . . . Speculation was a waste of time; he must wait until there was more evidence.

'Please fasten your seatbelts and secure all loose objects,' said the cabin speaker suddenly. 'Forty degree slope approaching.'

Two marker posts with winking lights had appeared on the horizon, and the bus was steering between them. Floyd had barely adjusted his straps when the vehicle slowly edged itself over the brink of a really terrifying incline, and began to descend a long, rubble-covered slope as steep as the roof of a house. The slanting earthlight, coming from behind them, now gave very little illumination, and the bus's own floodlights had been switched on. Many years ago, Floyd had stood on the lip of Vesuvius, staring into the crater; he could easily imagine that he was now driving down into it, and the sensation was not a very pleasant one.

They were descending one of the inner terraces of Tycho, and it levelled out again some thousand feet below. As they crawled down the slope, Michaels pointed out across the great expanse of plain now spread out beneath them.

'There they are,' he exclaimed. Floyd nodded; he had already noticed the cluster of red and green lights several miles ahead, and kept his eyes fixed upon it as the bus edged its way delicately down the slope. The big vehicle was obviously under perfect control, but he did not breathe easily until it was once more on an even keel.

Now he could see, glistening like silver bubbles in the earthlight, a group of pressure domes—the temporary shelters housing the workers on the site. Near these was a radio tower, a drilling rig, a group of parked vehicles, and a large pile of broken rock, presumably the material that had been excavated to reveal the monolith. This tiny camp in the wilderness looked very lonely, very vulnerable to the forces of nature ranged silently around it. There was no sign of life, and no visible hint as to why men had come here, so far from home.

'You can just see the crater,' said Michaels. 'Over there on the right—about a hundred yards from that radio antenna.'

So this is it, thought Floyd as the bus rolled past the pressure domes, and came to the lip of the crater. His pulse quickened, as he craned forward for a better view. The vehicle began to creep cautiously down a ramp of hard-packed rock, into the interior of the crater. And there, exactly as he had seen it in the photographs, was T.M.A.-1.

Floyd stared, blinked, shook his head, and stared again. Even in the brilliant earthlight, it was hard to see the object clearly; his first impression was a flat rectangle, that might have been cut out of carbon paper; it seemed to have no thickness at all. Of course, this was an optical illusion; though he was looking at a solid body, it reflected so little light that he could see it only in silhouette.

The passengers were utterly silent as the bus descended into the crater. There was awe, and there was also incredulity—sheer disbelief that the dead Moon, of all worlds, could have sprung this fantastic surprise.

The bus came to a halt within twenty feet of the slab, and broadside on so that all the passengers could examine it. Yet, beyond the geometrically perfect shape of the thing, there was little to see. Nowhere were there any marks, or any abatement of its ultimate, ebon blackness. It was the very crystallisation of night, and for one moment Floyd wondered if it could indeed be some extraordinary natural formation, born of the fires and pressures attending the creation of the Moon. But that remote possibility, he knew, had already been examined and dismissed.

At some signal, floodlights around the lip of the crater were switched on, and the bright earthlight was obliterated by a far more brilliant glare. In the lunar vacuum the beams were, of course, completely invisible; they formed overlapping ellipses of blinding white, centred on the monolith.

And where they touched it, its ebon surface seemed to swallow them.

Pandora's Box, thought Floyd, with a sudden sense of foreboding—waiting to be opened by inquisitive Man. And what will he find inside?

13

The Slow Dawn

The main pressure-dome at the T.M.A.-1 site was only twenty feet across, and its interior was uncomfortably crowded. The bus, coupled to it through one of the two airlocks, gave some much-appreciated extra living room.

Inside this hemispherical, double-walled balloon lived, worked and slept the six scientists and technicians now permanently attached to the project. It also contained most of their equipment and instruments, all the stores that could not be left in the vacuum outside, cooking, washing and toilet facilities, geological samples and a small TV screen through which the site could be kept under continuous surveillance.

Floyd was not surpised when Halvorsen elected to remain in the dome; he stated his views with admirable frankness.

'I regard spacesuits as a necessary evil,' said the Administrator. 'I wear one four times a year, for my quarterly checkout tests. If you don't mind, I'll sit here and watch over the TV.'

Some of this prejudice was now unjustified, for the latest models were infinitely more comfortable than the clumsy suits of armour worn by the first lunar explorers. They could be put on in less than a minute, even without help, and were quite automatic. The Mk. V into which Floyd was now carefully sealed would protect him from the worst that the Moon could do, either by day or by night.

Accompanied by Dr. Michaels, he walked into the small airlock. As the throbbing of the pumps died away, and his suit stiffened almost imperceptibly around him, he felt himself enclosed in the silence of vacuum.

That silence was broken by the welcome sound of his suit radio.

'Pressure O.K., Dr. Floyd? Are you breathing normally?'

'Yes—I'm fine.'

His companion carefully checked the dials and gauges on the outside of Floyd's suit. Then he said: 'O.K.—let's go.'

The outer door opened, and the dusty moonscape lay before them, glimmering in the earthlight.

With a cautious, waddling movement, Floyd followed Michaels through the lock. It was not hard to walk; indeed, in a paradoxical way the suit made him feel more at home than any time since reaching the Moon. Its extra weight, and the slight resistance it imposed on his motion, gave some of the illusion of the lost terrestrial gravity.

The scene had changed since the party had arrived barely an hour ago. Though the stars, and the half-earth, were still as bright as ever, the fourteen-day lunar night had almost ended. The glow of the corona was like a false moonrise along the eastern sky—and then, without warning, the tip of the radio mast a hundred feet above Floyd's head suddenly seemed to burst into flame, as it caught the first rays of the hidden Sun.

They waited while the project supervisor and two of his assistants emerged from the airlock, then walked slowly towards the crater. By the time they had reached it, a thin bow of unbearable incandescence had thrust itself above the eastern horizon. Though it would take more than an hour for the Sun to clear the edge of the slowly turning Moon, the stars were already banished.

The crater was still in shadow, but the floodlights mount-

ed around its rim lit the interior brilliantly. As Floyd walked
slowly down the ramp, towards the black rectangle, he felt
a sense not only of awe but of helplessness. Here, at the very
portals of Earth, man was already face to face with a mystery
that might never be solved. Three million years ago, *something* had passed this way, had left this unknown and perhaps
unknowable symbol of its purpose, and had returned to the
planets—or to the stars.

Floyd's suit radio interrupted his reverie. 'Project supervisor speaking. If you'd all line up on this side, we'd like to
take a few photos. Dr. Floyd, will you stand in the middle—
Dr. Michaels—thank you . . .'

No one except Floyd seemed to think that there was
anything funny about this. In all honesty he had to admit
that he was glad someone had brought a camera; here was
a photo that would undoubtedly be historic, and he wanted
copies for himself. He hoped that his face would be clearly
visible through the helmet of the suit.

'Thanks, gentlemen,' said the photographer, after they
had posed somewhat self-consciously in front of the monolith, and he had made a dozen exposures. 'We'll ask the
Base Photo Section to send you copies.'

Then Floyd turned his full attention to the ebon slab—
walking slowly around it, examining it from every angle,
trying to imprint its strangeness upon his mind. He did
not expect to find anything, for he knew that every square
inch had already been gone over with microscopic care.

Now the sluggish Sun had lifted itself above the edge of
the crater, and its rays were pouring almost broadside upon
the eastern side of the block. Yet it seemed to absorb every
particle of light as if it had never been.

Floyd decided to try a simple experiment; he stood between the monolith and the Sun, and looked for his own
shadow on the smooth black sheet. There was no trace of it.
At least ten kilowatts of raw heat must be falling on the slab;
if there was anything inside, it must be rapidly cooking.

How strange, Floyd thought, to stand here while this —this *thing*—is seeing daylight for the first time since the Ice Ages began on Earth. He wondered again about its black colour; that was ideal, of course, for absorbing solar energy. But he dismissed the thought at once; for who would be crazy enough to bury a sun-powered device twenty feet *underground*?

He looked up at the Earth, beginning to wane in the morning sky. Only a handful of the six billion people there knew of this discovery; how would the world react to the news when it was finally released?

The political and social implications were immense; every person of real intelligence—everyone who looked an inch beyond his nose—would find his life, his values, his philosophy, subtly changed. Even if nothing whatsoever was discovered about T.M.A.-1, and it remained an eternal mystery, Man would know that he was not unique in the universe. Though he had missed them by millions of years, those who had once stood here might yet return: and if not, there might well be others. All futures must now contain this possibility.

Floyd was still musing over these thoughts when his helmet speaker suddenly emitted a piercing electronic shriek, like a hideously overloaded and distorted time signal. Involuntarily, he tried to block his ears with his space-suited hands; then he recovered, and groped frantically for the gain control of his receiver. While he was still fumbling, four more of the shrieks blasted out of the ether; then there was a merciful silence.

All around the crater, figures were standing in attitudes of paralysed astonishment. So it's nothing wrong with *my* gear, Floyd told himself; everyone heard those piercing electronic screams.

After three million years of darkness T.M.A.-1 had greeted the lunar dawn.

14

The Listeners

A hundred million miles beyond Mars, in the cold loneliness where no man had yet travelled, Deep Space Monitor
79 drifted among the tangled orbits of the asteroids. For
three years it had fulfilled its mission flawlessly—a tribute
to the American scientists who had designed it, the British
engineers who had built it, the Russian technicians who
had launched it. A delicate spider's web of antennae sampled
the passing waves of radio noise—the ceaseless crackle and
hiss of what Pascal, in a far simpler age, had naively called
the 'silence of infinite space'. Radiation detectors noted and
analysed incoming cosmic rays from the Galaxy and points
beyond; neutron and X-ray telescopes kept watch on the
strange stars that no human eye would ever see; magnet-
ometers observed the gusts and hurricanes of the solar
winds, as the Sun breathed million-mile-an-hour blasts of
tenuous plasma into the faces of its circling children. All
these things, and many others, were patiently noted by
Deep Space Monitor 79, and recorded in its crystalline
memory.

One of its antennas, by now unconsidered miracles of
electronics, was always aimed at a point never far from
the Sun. Every few months its distant target could have
been seen, had there been any eye here to watch, as a bright
star with a close, fainter companion; but most of the time
it was lost in the solar glare.

To that far-off planet Earth, every twenty-four hours, the
monitor would send the information it had patiently gar-
nered, packed neatly into one five-minute pulse. About a
quarter of an hour later, travelling at the speed of light,
that pulse would reach its destination. The machines whose
duty it was would be waiting for it; they would amplify and

record the signal, and add it to the thousands of miles of magnetic tape now stored in the vaults of the World Space Centres at Washington, Moscow and Canberra.

Since the first satellites had orbited, almost fifty years earlier, billions and quadrillions of pulses of information had been pouring down from space, to be stored against the day when they might contribute to the advance of knowledge. Only a minute fraction of all this raw material would ever be processed; but there was no way of telling what observation some scientist might wish to consult, ten, or fifty, or a hundred years from now. So everything had to be kept on file, stacked in endless air-conditioned galleries, triplicated at the three centres against the possibility of accidental loss. It was part of the real treasure of mankind, more valuable than all the gold locked uselessly away in bank vaults.

And now Deep Space Monitor 79 had noted something strange—a faint yet unmistakable disturbance rippling across the Solar System, and quite unlike any natural phenomenon it had ever observed in the past. Automatically, it recorded the direction, the time, the intensity; in a few hours it would pass the information to Earth.

As, also, would Orbiter M 15, circling Mars twice a day; and High Inclination Probe 21, climbing slowly above the plane of the ecliptic; and even Artificial Comet 5, heading out into the cold wastes beyond Pluto, along an orbit whose far point it would not reach for a thousand years. All noted the peculiar burst of energy that had disturbed their instruments; all, in due course, reported back automatically to the memory stores on distant Earth.

The computers might never have perceived the connection between four peculiar sets of signals, from space-probes on independent orbits millions of miles apart. But as soon as he glanced at his morning report, the Radiation Forecaster at Goddard knew that something strange had passed through the Solar System during the last twenty-four hours.

He had only part of its track, but when the computer projected it on the Planet Situation Board, it was as clear and unmistakable as a vapour trail across a cloudless sky, or a single line of footprints over a field of virgin snow. Some immaterial pattern of energy, throwing off a spray of radiation like the wake of a racing speedboat, had leaped from the face of the Moon, and was heading out towards the stars.

III

BETWEEN PLANETS

15

'Discovery'

The ship was still only thirty days from Earth; yet David Bowman sometimes found it hard to believe that he had ever known any other existence than the closed little world of *Discovery*. All his years of training, all his earlier missions to the Moon and Mars, seemed to belong to another man, in another life.

Frank Poole admitted to the same feelings, and had sometimes jokingly regretted that the nearest psychiatrist was the better part of a hundred million miles away. But this sense of isolation and estrangement was easy enough to understand, and certainly indicated no abnormality. In the fifty years since men had ventured into space, there had never been a mission quite like this.

It had begun, five years ago, as Project Jupiter—the first manned round trip to the greatest of the planets. The ship was nearly ready for the two-year voyage when, somewhat abruptly, the mission profile had been changed.

Discovery would still go to Jupiter; but she would not stop there. She would not even slacken speed as she raced through the far-ranging Jovian satellite system. On the contrary—she would use the gravitational field of the giant world as a sling, to cast her even further from the Sun. Like a comet, she would streak on across the outer reaches of the Solar System to her ultimate goal, the ringed glory of Saturn. And she would never return.

For *Discovery*, it would be a one-way trip—yet her crew had no intention of committing suicide. If all went well,

they would be back on Earth within seven years—five of
which would pass like a flash in the dreamless sleep of
hibernation, while they awaited rescue by the still unbuilt
Discovery II.

The word 'rescue' was carefully avoided in all the Astronautics Agencies' statements and documents; it implied
some failure of planning, and the approved jargon was
'reacquisition'. If anything went really wrong, there would
certainly be no hope of rescue, almost a billion miles from
Earth.

It was a calculated risk, like all voyages into the unknown.
But half a century of research had proved that artificially-
induced human hibernation was perfectly safe, and it
had opened up new possibilities in space-travel. Not until
this mission, however, had they been exploited to the
utmost.

The three members of the survey team, who would not
be needed until the ship entered her final orbit around
Saturn, would sleep through the entire outward flight. Tons
of food and other expendables would thus be saved; almost
as important, the team would be fresh and alert, and not
fatigued by the ten-month voyage, when they went into
action.

Discovery would enter a parking orbit around Saturn,
becoming a new moon of the giant planet. She would swing
back and forth along a two-million-mile ellipse that took
her close to Saturn, and then across the orbits of all its
major moons. They would have a hundred days in which
to map and study a world with eighty times the area of
Earth, and surrounded by a retinue of at least fifteen known
satellites—one of them as large as the planet Mercury.

There must be wonders enough here for centuries of study;
the first expedition could only carry out a preliminary reconnaissance. All that it found would be radioed back to
Earth; even if the explorers never returned, their discoveries
would not be lost.

At the end of the hundred days *Discovery* would close down. All the crew would go into hibernation; only the essential systems would continue to operate, watched over by the ship's tireless electronic brain. She would continue to swing around Saturn, on an orbit now so well determined that men would know exactly where to look for her a thousand years hence. But in only five years, according to present plans, *Discovery II* would come. Even if six, or seven or eight years elapsed her sleeping passengers would never know the difference. For all of them, the clock would have stopped—as it had stopped already for Whitehead, Kaminski and Hunter.

Sometimes Bowman, as First Captain of *Discovery*, envied his three unconscious colleagues in the frozen peace of the Hibernaculum. They were free from all boredom and all responsibility; until they reached Saturn, the external world did not exist.

But that world was watching them, through their bio-sensor displays. Tucked inconspicuously away among the massed instrumentation of the Control Deck were five small panels marked HUNTER, WHITEHEAD, KAMINSKI, POOLE, BOWMAN. The last two were blank and lifeless; their time would not come until a year from now. The others bore constellations of tiny green lights, announcing that everything was well; and on each was a small display screen across which sets of glowing lines traced the leisurely rhythms that indicated pulse, respiration and brain activity.

There were times when Bowman, well aware how un-necessary this was—for the alarm would sound instantly if anything was wrong—would switch over to audio output. He would listen, half hypnotised, to the infinitely slow heart-beats of his sleeping colleagues, keeping his eyes fixed on the sluggish waves that marched in synchronism across the screen.

Most fascinating of all were the E.E.G. displays—the electronic signatures of three personalities that had once existed, and would one day exist again. They were almost free from the spikes and valleys, the electrical explosions that marked the activity of the waking brain—or even of the brain in normal sleep. If there was any wisp of consciousness remaining, it was beyond the reach of instruments, and of memory.

This last fact, Bowman knew from personal experience. Before he was chosen for this mission, his reactions to hibernation had been tested. He was not sure whether he had lost a week of his life—or whether he had postponed his eventual death by the same amount of time.

When the electrodes had been attached to his forehead, and the sleep-generator had started to pulse, he had seen a brief display of kaleidoscopic patterns and drifting stars. Then they had faded, and darkness had engulfed him. He had never felt the injections, still less the first touch of cold as his body temperature was reduced to only a few degrees above freezing. . . .

.

. . . He awoke, and it seemed that he had scarcely closed his eyes. But he knew that was an illusion; somehow, he was convinced that years had really passed.

Had the mission been completed? Had they already reached Saturn, carried out their survey, and gone into hibernation? Was *Discovery II* here, to take them back to Earth?

He lay in a dream-like daze, utterly unable to distinguish between real and false memories. He opened his eyes, but there was little to see except a blurred constellation of lights which puzzled him for some minutes. Then he realised that he was looking at the indicator lamps on a Ship Situation Board; but it was impossible to focus on them. He soon gave up the attempt.

Warm air was blowing across him, removing the chill from his limbs. There was quiet, but stimulating music welling from a speaker behind his head. It was slowly growing louder and louder . . .

Then a relaxed, friendly—but, he knew, computer-generated—voice spoke to him.

'You are becoming operational, Dave. Do not get up or attempt any violent movements. Do not try to speak.'

Do not get up! thought Bowman. *That* was funny. He doubted if he could wriggle a finger. Rather to his surprise, he found that he could.

He felt quite contented, in a dazed, stupid kind of way. He knew dimly that the rescue ship must have come, that the automatic revival sequence had been triggered, soon he would be seeing other human beings. That was fine, but he did not get excited about it.

Presently he felt hunger. The computer, of course, had anticipated this need.

'There is a signal button by your right hand, Dave. If you are hungry, please press it.'

Bowman forced his fingers to hunt around, and presently discovered the pear-shaped bulb. He had forgotten all about it, though he must have known it was there. How much else had he forgotten—did hibernation erase memory?

He pressed the button, and waited. Several minutes later, a metal arm moved out from the bunk, and a plastic nipple descended towards his lips. He sucked on it eagerly, and a warm, sweet fluid coursed down his throat, bringing renewed strength with every drop.

Presently it went away, and he rested once more. He could move his arms and legs now; the thought of walking was no longer an impossible dream.

Though he felt his strength swiftly returning, he would have been content to lie here for ever, if there had been no further stimulus from outside. But presently another voice spoke to him—and this time it was wholly human, not a construct of electrical pulses assembled by a more-than-human memory. It was also a familiar voice, though it was some time before he could recognise it.

'Hello, Dave. You're coming round fine. You can talk now. Do you know where you are?'

He worried about this for some time. If he was *really* orbiting Saturn, what had happened during all the months since he had left Earth? Again he began to wonder if he was suffering from amnesia. Paradoxically, the very thought reassured him. If he could remember the word 'amnesia', his brain must be in fairly good shape. . . .

But he still did not know where he was, and the speaker at the other end of the circuit must have understood his situation completely.

'Don't worry, Dave. This is Frank Poole. I'm watching your heart and respiration—everything is perfectly normal. Just relax—take it easy. We're going to open the door now and pull you out.'

Soft light flooded into the chamber; he saw moving shapes silhouetted against the widening entrance. And in that moment, all his memories came back to him, and he knew exactly where he was.

Though he had come back safely from the furthest borders of sleep, and the nearest borders of death, he had been gone only a week. When he left the hibernaculum, he would not see the cold Saturnian sky; that was more than a year in the future and half a billion miles away. He was still in the crew trainer at the Houston Space Flight Center, under the hot Texas sun.

16

Hal

But now Texas was invisible, and even the United States was hard to see. Though the low-thrust plasma drive had long since been closed down, *Discovery* was still coasting with her slender, arrow-like body pointed away from Earth, and all her high-powered optical gear was orientated towards the outer planets, where her destiny lay.

There was one telescope, however, that was permanently aimed at Earth. It was mounted like a gunsight on the rim of the ship's long-range antenna, and checked that the great parabolic bowl was rigidly locked upon its distant target. While Earth remained centred in the crosswires, the vital communication link was intact, and messages could come and go along the invisible beam that lengthened more than two million miles with every day that passed.

At least once in every watch period, Bowman would look homeward through the antenna-alignment telescope. As Earth was now far back towards the Sun, its darkened hemisphere faced *Discovery*, and on the central display screen the planet appeared as a dazzling silver crescent, like another Venus.

It was rare that any geographical features could be identified, in that ever-shrinking arc of light, for cloud and haze concealed them, but even the darkened portion of the disc was endlessly fascinating. It was sprinkled with shining cities; sometimes they burned with a steady light, sometimes they twinkled like fireflies as atmospheric tremors passed over them.

There were also periods when, as the Moon swung back and forth in its orbit, it shone down like a great lamp upon the darkened seas and continents of Earth. Then, with a thrill of recognition, Bowman could often glimpse familiar coastlines, shining in that spectral lunar light. And sometimes, when the Pacific was calm, he could even see the moonglow shimmering across its face; and he would remember nights beneath the palm trees of tropical lagoons.

Yet he had no regrets for these lost beauties. He had enjoyed them all, in his thirty-five years of life; and he was determined to enjoy them again, when he returned rich and famous. Meanwhile, distance made them all the more precious.

The sixth member of the crew cared for none of these things, for it was not human. It was the highly advanced HAL 9000 computer, the brain and nervous system of the ship.

Hal (for *H*euristically programmed *AL*gorithmic computer, no less) was a masterwork of the third computer breakthrough. These seemed to occur at intervals of twenty years, and the thought that another one was now imminent already worried a great many people.

The first had been in the 1940's, when the long-obsolete vacuum tube had made possible such clumsy, high-speed morons as ENIAC and its successors. Then, in the 1960's, solid-state microelectronics had been perfected. With their advent, it was clear that artificial intelligences at least as powerful as Man's need be no larger than office desks—if one only knew how to construct them.

Probably no one would ever know this; it did not matter. In the 1980's, Minsky and Good had shown how neural networks could be generated automatically—self-replicated —in accordance with any arbitrary learning programme. Artificial brains could be grown by a process strikingly analogous to the development of a human brain. In any given case, the precise details would never be known, and even if they were, they would be millions of times too complex for human understanding.

Whatever way it worked, the final result was a machine intelligence that could reproduce—some philosophers still preferred to use the word 'mimic'—most of the activities of the human brain, and with far greater speed and reliability. It was extremely expensive, and only a few units of the HAL 9000 series had yet been built; but the old jest that it would always be easier to make organic brains by unskilled labour was beginning to sound a little hollow.

Hal had been trained for this mission as thoroughly as his human colleagues—and at many times their rate of input, for in addition to his instrinsic speed, he never slept. His prime task was to monitor the life-support systems, continually checking oxygen pressure, temperature, hull leakage, radiation and all the other interlocking factors upon which the lives of the fragile human cargo depended. He could carry out the intricate navigational corrections, and execute the necessary flight manœuvres when it was time to change course. And he could watch over the hibernators, making any necessary adjustments to their environment, and doling out the minute quantities of intravenous fluids that kept them alive.

The first generations of computers had received their inputs through glorified typewriter keyboards, and had replied through high-speed printers and visual displays. Hal could do this when necessary, but most of his communication with his shipmates was by means of the spoken word. Poole and Bowman could talk to Hal as if he were a human being, and he would reply in the perfect, idiomatic English he had learned during the fleeting weeks of his electronic childhood.

Whether Hal could actually think was a question which had been settled by the British mathematician Alan Turing back in the 1940's. Turing had pointed out that, if one could carry out a prolonged conversation with a machine—whether by typewriter or microphone was immaterial—without being able to distinguish between its replies and those that a man might give, then the machine *was* thinking, by any sensible definition of the word. Hal could pass the Turing test with ease.

The time might even come when Hal would take command of the ship. In an emergency, if no one answered his signals, he would attempt to wake the sleeping members of the crew, by electrical and chemical stimulation. If they did not respond, he would radio Earth for further orders.

And then, if there was no reply from Earth, he would take what measures he deemed necessary to safeguard the ship and to continue the mission—whose real purpose he alone knew, and which his human colleagues could never have guessed.

Poole and Bowman had often humorously referred to themselves as caretakers or janitors aboard a ship that could really run itself. They would have been astonished, and more than a little indignant, to discover how much truth that jest contained.

17

Cruise Mode

The day-by-day running of the ship had been planned with great care, and—theoretically at least—Bowman and Poole knew what they would be doing at every moment of the twenty-four hours. They operated on a twelve-hours-on, twelve-hours-off basis, taking charge alternately, and never being both asleep at the same time. The officer-on-duty normally remained on the Control Deck, while his deputy saw to the general housekeeping, inspected the ship, coped with the odd jobs that constantly arose, or relaxed in his cubicle.

Although Bowman was nominal captain, on this phase of the mission no outside observer could have deduced the fact. He and Poole switched roles, rank and responsibilities completely every twelve hours. This kept them both at peak training, minimised the chances of friction, and helped towards the goal of a hundred per cent redundancy.

Bowman's day began at 1600, Ship's Time—the Universal Ephemeris Time of the astronomers. If he was late, Hal had a variety of beeps and chimes to remind him of his duty, but they had never been used. As a test, Poole had once switched off the alarm; Bowman had still risen automatically at the right time.

His first official act of the day would be to advance the Master Hibernation Timer twelve hours. If this operation was missed twice in a row, Hal would assume that both he and Poole had been incapacitated, and would take the necessary emergency action.

Bowman would attend to his toilet, and do his isometric exercises, before settling down to breakfast and the morning's radio-fax edition of the *World Times*. On Earth he never read the paper as carefully as he did now; even the smallest items of society gossip, the most fleeting political rumours, seemed of absorbing interest as it flashed across the screen.

At 0700 he would officially relieve Poole on the Control Deck, bringing him a squeeze-tube of coffee from the kitchen. If—as was usually the case—there was nothing to report and no action to be taken, he would settle down to check all the instrument readings, and would run through a series of tests designed to spot possible malfunctions. By 1000 this would be finished, and he would start on a study period.

Bowman had been a student for more than half his life; he would continue to be one until he retired. Thanks to the Twentieth Century revolution in training and information-handling techniques, he already possessed the equivalent of two or three college educations—and, what was more, he could remember 90 per cent of what he had learned.

Fifty years ago, he would have been considered a specialist in applied astronomy, cybernetics and space propulsion

systems—yet he was prone to deny, with genuine indigna-
tion, that he was a specialist at all. Bowman had never found
it possible to focus his interest exclusively on any subject;
despite the dark-warnings of his instructors, he had insisted
on taking his Master's degree in General Astronautics—a
course with a vague and woolly syllabus, designed for those
whose I.Q.s were in the low 130s, and who would never
reach to the top ranks of their profession.

His decision had been right; that very refusal to specialise
had made him uniquely qualified for his present task. In
much the same way Frank Poole—who sometimes disparag-
ingly called himself 'General Practitioner in space biology'
—had been an ideal choice as his deputy. The two of them,
with, if necessary, help from Hal's vast stores of information, could cope with any problems likely to arise during the
voyage—as long as they kept their minds alert and receptive,
and continually re-engraved old patterns of memory.

So for two hours, from 1000 to 1200, Bowman would
engage in a dialogue with an electronic tutor, checking his
general knowledge or absorbing material specific to this
mission. He would prowl endlessly over ship's plans, circuit
diagrams and voyage profiles, or would try to assimilate all
that was known about Jupiter, Saturn and their far-ranging
families of moons.

At midday, he would retire to the galley and leave the
ship to Hal while he prepared his lunch. Even here, he was
still fully in touch with events, for the tiny lounge-cum-
dining-room contained a duplicate of the Situation Display
Panel, and Hal could call him at a moment's notice. Poole
would join him for this meal, before retiring for his six-hour
sleep period, and usually they would watch one of the regular
TV programmes beamed to them from Earth.

Their menus had been planned with as much care as any
part of the mission. The food, most of it freeze-dried, was
uniformly excellent, and had been chosen for the minimum
of trouble. Packets had merely to be opened and popped

into the tiny auto-galley, which beeped for attention when the job was done. They could enjoy what tasted like—and, equally important, *looked* like—orange juice, eggs (any style), steaks, chops, roasts, fresh vegetables, assorted fruits, ice-cream, and even freshly-baked bread.

After lunch, from 1300 to 1600, Bowman would make a slow and careful tour of the ship—or such part of it as was accessible. *Discovery* measured almost four hundred feet from end to end, but the little universe occupied by her crew lay entirely inside the forty-foot sphere of the pressure hull.

Here were all the life-support systems, and the Control Deck which was the operational heart of the ship. Below this was a small 'space-garage' fitted with three airlocks through which powered capsules, just large enough to hold a man, could sail out into the void if the need arose for extra-vehicular activity.

The equatorial region of the pressure-sphere—the slice, as it were, from Capricorn to Cancer—enclosed a slowly-rotating drum, thirty-five feet in diameter. As it made one revolution every ten seconds, this carousel or centrifuge produced an artificial gravity equal to that of the Moon. This was enough to prevent the physical atrophy which would result from the complete absence of weight, and it also allowed the routine functions of living to be carried out under normal—or nearly normal—conditions.

The carousel therefore contained the kitchen, dining, washing and toilet facilities. Only here was it safe to prepare and handle hot drinks—quite dangerous in weightless conditions, where one can be badly scalded by floating globules of boiling water. The problem of shaving was also solved; there would be no weightless bristles drifting around, to endanger electrical equipment and produce a health hazard.

Around the rim of the carousel were five tiny cubicles, fitted out by each astronaut according to taste and containing his personal belongings. Only Bowman's and Poole's were now in use, while the future occupants of the other three cabins reposed in their electronic sarcophagi next door.

The spin of the carousel could be stopped if necessary; when this happened, its angular momentum had to be stored in a flywheel, and switched back again when rotation was re-started. But normally it was left running at constant speed, for it was easy enough to enter the big, slowly turning drum by going hand-over-hand along a pole through the zero-gee region at its centre. Transferring to the moving section was as easy and automatic, after a little experience, as stepping on to a moving escalator.

The spherical pressure-hull formed the head of a flimsy, arrow-shaped structure more than a hundred yards long. *Discovery*, like all vehicles intended for deep-space penetration, was too fragile and unstreamlined ever to enter an atmosphere, or to defy the full gravitational field of any planet. She had been assembled in orbit around the Earth, tested on a translunar maiden flight, and finally checked out in orbit above the Moon. She was a creature of pure space— and she looked it.

Immediately behind the pressure-hull was grouped a cluster of four large liquid hydrogen tanks—and beyond them, forming a long, slender Vee, were the radiating fins that dissipated the waste heat of the nuclear reactor. Veined with a delicate tracery of pipes for the cooling fluid, they looked like the wings of some vast dragonfly, and from certain angles gave *Discovery* a fleeting resemblance to an old-time sailing ship.

At the very end of the Vee, three hundred feet from the crew-compartment, was the shielded inferno of the reactor, and the complex of focussing electrodes through which emerged the incandescent star-stuff of the plasma drive. This had done its work weeks ago, forcing *Discovery* out of her parking orbit round the Moon. Now the reactor was merely ticking over as it generated electrical power for the ship's services, and the great radiating fins, that would glow cherry red when *Discovery* was accelerating under maximum thrust, were dark and cool.

Although it would require an excursion out into space to examine this region of the ship, there were instruments and remote TV cameras which gave a full report on conditions here. Bowman now felt that he knew intimately every square foot of radiator panels, and every piece of plumbing associated with them.

By 1600, he would have finished his inspection, and would make a detailed verbal report to Mission Control, talking until the acknowledgement started to come in. Then he would switch off his own transmitter, listen to what Earth had to say, and send back his reply to any queries. At 1800 hours, Poole would awaken, and he would hand over command.

He would then have six off-duty hours, to use as he pleased. Sometimes he could continue his studies, or listen to music, or look at movies. Much of the time he would wander at will through the ship's inexhaustible electronic library. He had become fascinated by the great explorations of the past—understandably enough, in the circumstances. Sometimes he would cruise with Pytheas out through the Pillars of Hercules, along the coast of a Europe barely emerging from the Stone Age, and venture almost to the chill mists of the Arctic. Or two thousand years later, he would pursue the Manilla galleons with Anson, sail with Cook along the unknown hazards of the Great Barrier Reef, achieve with Magellan the first circumnavigation of the world. And he began to read the Odyssey, which of all books spoke to him most vividly across the gulfs of time.

For relaxation he could always engage Hal in a large number of semi-mathematical games, including checkers, chess and pantominoes. If Hal went all out, he could win any one of them; but that would be bad for morale. So he had been programmed to win only fifty per cent of the time, and his human partners pretended not to know this.

The last hours of Bowman's day were devoted to general cleaning up and odd jobs, followed by dinner at 2000— again with Poole. Then there would be an hour during which he would make or receive any personal calls from Earth.

Like all his colleagues, Bowman was unmarried; it was not fair to send family men on a mission of such duration. Though numerous ladies had promised to wait until the expedition returned, no one had really believed this. At first, both Poole and Bowman had been making rather intimate personal calls once a week, though the knowledge that many ears must be listening at the Earth end of the circuit tended to inhibit them. Yet already, though the voyage was scarcely started, the warmth and frequency of the conversations with their girls on Earth had begun to diminish. They had expected this; it was one of the penalties of an astronaut's, as it had once been of a mariner's way of life.

It was true—indeed, notorious—that seamen had compensations at other ports; unfortunately there were no tropical islands full of dusky maids beyond the orbit of Earth. The space medics, of course, had tackled this problem with their usual enthusiasm; and the ship's pharmacopœia provided adequate, though hardly glamorous, substitutes.

Just before he signed off, Bowman would make his final report, and check that Hal had transmitted all the instrumentation tapes for the day's run. Then, if he felt like it, he would spend a couple of hours either reading or looking at a movie; and at midnight, he would go to sleep—usually without any help from electronarcosis.

Poole's programme was a mirror image of his own, and the two schedules dovetailed together without friction. Both men were fully occupied, they were too intelligent and well adjusted to quarrel, and the voyage had settled down to a comfortable, utterly uneventful routine, the passage of time marked only by the changing numbers on the digital clocks.

The greatest hope of *Discovery*'s little crew was that nothing would mar this peaceful monotony, in the weeks and months that lay ahead.

18

Through the Asteroids

Week after week, running like a streetcar along the tracks of her utterly predetermined orbit, *Discovery* swept past the orbit of Mars and on towards Jupiter. Unlike all the vessels traversing the skies or seas of Earth, she required not even the most minute touch on the controls. Her course was fixed by the laws of gravitation; there were no uncharted shoals, no dangerous reefs on which she would run aground. Nor was there the slightest danger of collision with another ship; for there was no vessel—at least of Man's making—anywhere between her and the infinitely distant stars.

Yet the space which she was now entering was far from empty. Ahead lay a no-man's-land threaded by the paths of more than a million asteroids—less than ten thousand of which had ever had their orbits precisely determined by astronomers. Only four were over a hundred miles in diameter; the vast majority were merely giant boulders, trundling aimlessly through space.

There was nothing that could be done about them; though even the smallest could completely destroy the ship if it slammed into it at tens of thousands of miles an hour, the chance of this happening was negligible. On the average, there was only one asteroid in a volume a million miles on a side; that *Discovery* should also happen to occupy this same point, and *at the same time*, was the very least of her crew's worries.

On Day 86 they were due to make their closest approach to any known asteroid. It had no name—merely the number 7794—and was a fifty-yard-diameter rock that had been detected by the Lunar Observatory in 1997 and immediately forgotten except by the patient computers of the Minor Planet Bureau.

When Bowman came on duty, Hal promptly reminded him of the forthcoming encounter—not that he was likely to have forgotten the only scheduled in-flight event of the entire voyage. The track of the asteroids against the stars, and its co-ordinates at the moment of closest approach, had already been printed out on the display screens. Listed also were the observations to be made or attempted; they were going to be very busy when 7794 flashed past them only nine hundred miles away, at a relative speed of eighty thousand miles an hour.

When Bowman asked Hal for the telescopic display, a sparsely sprinkled star field flashed on to the screen. There was nothing that looked like an asteroid; all the images, even under the highest magnification, were dimensionless points of light.

'Give me the target reticule,' asked Bowman. Immediately four faint, narrow lines appeared, bracketing a tiny and undistinguished star. He stared at it for many minutes, wondering if Hal could possibly be mistaken; then he saw that the pinpoint of light was moving, with barely perceptible slowness, against the background of the stars. It might still be half a million miles away—but its movement proved that, as cosmic distances went, it was almost near enough to touch.

When Poole joined him on the Control Deck, six hours later, 7794 was hundreds of times more brilliant, and was moving so swiftly against its background that there was no question of its identity. And it was no longer a point of light; it had begun to show a clearly visible disc.

They stared at that passing pebble in the sky with the

emotions of sailors on a long sea voyage, skirting a coast on which they cannot land. Though they were perfectly well aware that 7794 was only a lifeless, airless chunk of rock, this knowledge scarcely affected their feelings. It was the only solid matter they would meet this side of Jupiter—still two hundred million miles away.

Through the high-powered telescope, they could see that the asteroid was very irregular, and turning slowly end over end. Sometimes it looked like a flattened sphere, sometimes it resembled a roughly-shaped brick; its rotation period was just over two minutes. There were mottled patches of light and shade distributed apparently at random over its surface, and often it sparkled like a distant window as planes or outcroppings of crystalline material flashed in the Sun.

It was racing past them at almost thirty miles a second; they had only a few frantic minutes in which to observe it closely. The automatic cameras took dozens of photographs, the navigation radar's returning echoes were carefully re-corded for future analysis—and there was just time for a single impact probe.

The probe carried no instruments; none could survive a collision at such cosmic speeds. It was merely a small slug of metal, shot out from *Discovery* on a course which should intersect that of the asteroid.

As the seconds before impact ticked away, Poole and Bowman waited with mounting tension. The experiment, simple though it was in principle, taxed the accuracy of their equipment to the limits. They were aiming at a hundred-and-fifty-foot-diameter target, from a distance of thousands of miles. . . .

Against the darkened portion of the asteroid, there was a sudden, dazzling explosion of light. The tiny slug had impacted at meteoric speed; in a fraction of a second, all its energy had been transformed into heat. A puff of incan-descent gas had erupted briefly into space; aboard *Discovery*, the cameras were recording the rapidly-fading spectral lines. Back on Earth, experts would analyse them, looking for the tell-tale signatures of glowing atoms. And so, for the first time, the composition of an asteroid's crust would be determined.

Within an hour, 7794 was a dwindling star, showing no trace of a disc. When Bowman next came on watch it had vanished completely.

They were alone again; they would remain alone, until the outermost of Jupiter's moons came swimming up towards them, three months from now.

19

Transit of Jupiter

Even from twenty million miles away, Jupiter was already the most conspicuous object in the sky ahead. The planet was now a pale, salmon-hued disc, about half the size of the Moon as seen from Earth, with the dark, parallel bands of its cloud-belts clearly visible. Shuttling back and forth in the equatorial plane were the brilliant stars of Io, Europa, Ganymede and Callisto—worlds that elsewhere would have counted as planets in their own right, but which here were merely satellites of a giant master.

Through the telescope, Jupiter was a glorious sight—a mottled, multicoloured globe that seemed to fill the sky. It was impossible to grasp its real size; Bowman kept reminding himself that it was eleven times the diameter of Earth, but for a long time this was a statistic with no real meaning.

Then, while he was briefing himself from the tapes in Hal's memory units, he found something that suddenly brought the appalling scale of the planet into focus. It was an illustration that showed the Earth's entire surface peeled off and then pegged, like the skin of an animal, on the disc of Jupiter. Against *this* background, all the continents and oceans of Earth appeared no larger than India on the terrestrial globe. . . .

When Bowman used the highest magnification of *Discovery*'s telescopes, he appeared to be hanging above a slightly flattened globe, looking down upon a vista of racing clouds that had been smeared into bands by the giant world's swift rotation. Sometimes those bands congealed into wisps and knots and continent-sized masses of coloured vapour; sometimes they were linked by transient bridges thousands of miles in length. Hidden beneath those clouds was enough material to outweigh all the other planets in the Solar System. And what *else*, Bowman wondered, was also hidden there?

Over this shifting, turbulent roof of clouds, forever hiding the real surface of the planet, circular patterns of darkness sometimes glided. One of the inner moons was transiting the distant Sun, its shadow marching beneath it over the restless Jovian cloudscape.

There were other, and far smaller, moons even out here— twenty million miles from Jupiter. But they were only flying mountains a few dozen miles in diameter, and the ship would pass nowhere near any of them. Every few minutes, the radar transmitter would gather its strength and send out a silent thunderclap of power; no echoes of new satellites came pulsing back from the emptiness.

What did come, with ever-growing intensity, was the roar of Jupiter's own radio voice. In 1955, just before the dawn of the space age, astronomers had been astonished to find that Jupiter was blasting out millions of horsepower on the ten-metre band. It was merely raw noise, associated with haloes of charged particles circling the planet like the Van Allen Belts of Earth, but on a far greater scale.

Sometimes, during lonely hours on the Control Deck,

Bowman would listen to this radiation. He would turn up
the gain until the room filled with a crackling, sissing roar;
out of this background, at irregular intervals, emerged brief
whistles and peeps like the cries of demented birds. It was an
eerie sound, for it had nothing to do with Man; it was as
lonely and as meaningless as the murmur of waves on a
beach, or the distant crash of thunder beyond the horizon.

Even at her present speed of over a hundred thousand
miles an hour, it would take *Discovery* almost two weeks to
cross the orbits of all the Jovian satellites. More moons
circled Jupiter than planets orbited the Sun; the Lunar
Observatory was discovering new ones every year, and the
tally had now reached thirty-six. The outermost—Jupiter
XXVII—moved backwards in an unstable path nineteen
million miles from its temporary master. It was the prize in a
perpetual tug-of-war between Jupiter and the Sun, for the
planet was constantly capturing short-lived moons from the
asteroid belt, and losing them again after a few million
years. Only the inner satellites were its permanent property;
the Sun could never wrest them from its grasp.

Now there was new prey for the clashing gravitational
fields. *Discovery* was accelerating towards Jupiter along a
complex orbit computed months ago by the astronomers on
Earth, and constantly checked by Hal. From time to time
there would be minute, automatic nudges from the control
jets, scarcely perceptible aboard the ship, as they made fine
adjustment to the trajectory.

Over the radio link with Earth, information was flowing
back in a constant stream. They were now so far from home
that, even travelling at the speed of light, their signals were
taking fifty minutes for the journey. Though the whole
world was looking over their shoulders, watching through
their eyes and their instruments as Jupiter approached, it
would be almost an hour before the news of their discoveries
reached home.

The telescopic cameras were operating constantly as the

ship cut across the orbit of the giant inner satellites—every one of them larger than the Moon, every one of them unknown territory. Three hours before transit, *Discovery* passed only twenty thousand miles from Europa, and all instruments were aimed at the approaching world, as it grew steadily in size, changed from globe to crescent, and swept swiftly sunward.

Here were fourteen million square miles of land, which, until this moment, had never been more than a pinhead in the mightiest telescope. They would race past it in minutes, and must make the most of the encounter, recording all the information they could. There would be months in which they could play it back at leisure.

From a distance, Europa had seemed like a giant snowball, reflecting the light of the far-off Sun with remarkable efficiency. Closer observations confirmed this; unlike the dusty Moon, Europa was a brilliant white, and much of its surface was covered with glittering hunks that looked like stranded icebergs. Almost certainly, these were formed from ammonia and water that Jupiter's gravitational field had somehow failed to capture.

Only along the equator was bare rock visible; here was an incredibly jagged no-man's-land of canyons and jumbled boulders, forming a darker band that completely surrounded the little world. There were a few impact craters, but no sign of vulcanism; Europa had obviously never possessed any internal sources of heat.

There was, as had long been known, a trace of atmosphere. When the dark edge of the satellite passed across a star, it dimmed briefly before the moment of eclipse. And in some areas there was a hint of cloud—perhaps a mist of ammonia droplets, borne on tenuous methane winds.

As swiftly as it had rushed out of the sky ahead, Europa dropped astern; and now Jupiter itself was only two hours away. Hal had checked and rechecked the ship's orbit with infinite care, and there was no need for further speed corrections until the moment of closest approach. Yet, even knowing this, it was a strain on the nerves to watch that giant globe ballooning minute by minute. It was difficult to believe that *Discovery* was not plunging directly into it, that the planet's immense gravitational field was not dragging them down to destruction.

Now was the time to drop the atmospheric probes—which, it was hoped, would survive long enough to send back some information from below the Jovian cloud-deck. Two stubby, bomb-shaped capsules, enclosed in ablative heat-shields, were gently nudged into orbits which for the first few thousand miles deviated scarcely at all from that of *Discovery*.

But they slowly drifted away; and now, at last, even the unaided eye could see what Hal had been asserting. The ship was in a near-grazing orbit, not a collision one; she would miss the atmosphere. True, the difference was only a few hundred miles—a mere nothing, when one was dealing with a planet ninety thousand miles in diameter—but that was enough.

Jupiter now filled the entire sky; it was so huge that neither mind nor eye could grasp it any longer, and both had abandoned the attempt. If it had not been for the extraordinary variety of colour—the reds and pinks and yellows and salmons and even scarlets—of the atmosphere beneath them, Bowman could have believed that he was flying low over a cloudscape on Earth.

And now, for the first time in all their journeying, they were about to lose the Sun. Pale and shrunken though it was, it had been *Discovery*'s constant companion since her departure from Earth, five months ago. But now her orbit was diving into the shadow of Jupiter; she would soon pass over the night side of the planet.

A thousand miles ahead, the band of twilight was hurtling towards them; behind, the Sun was sinking swiftly into the Jovian clouds. Its rays spread out along the horizon like two flaming, down-turned horns, then contracted and died in a brief blaze of chromatic glory. The night had come.

And yet—the great world below was not wholly dark. It was awash with phosphorescence, which grew brighter minute by minute as their eyes grew accustomed to the scene. Dim rivers of light were flowing from horizon to horizon, like the luminous wakes of ships on some tropical sea. Here and there they gathered into pools of liquid fire, trembling with vast, submarine disturbances welling up from the hidden heart of Jupiter. It was a sight so awe-inspiring that Poole and Bowman could have stared for hours; was this, they wondered, merely the result of chemical and electrical forces down there in that seething cauldron—or was it the by-product of some fantastic form of life? These were questions which scientists might still be debating when the new-born century drew to its close.

As they drove deeper and deeper into the Jovian night, the glow beneath them grew steadily brighter. Once Bowman had flown over northern Canada during the height of an auroral display; the snow-covered landscape had been as bleak and brilliant as this. And *that* arctic wilderness, he reminded himself, was more than a hundred degrees warmer than the regions over which they were hurtling now.

'Earth signal is fading rapidly,' announced Hal. 'We are entering the first diffraction zone.'

They had expected this—indeed, it was one of the mission's objectives, as the absorption of radio waves would give valuable information about the Jovian atmosphere. But now that they had actually passed behind the planet, and it was cutting off communication with Earth, they felt a sudden overwhelming loneliness. The radio blackout would last only an hour; then they would emerge from Jupiter's eclipsing screen, and could resume contact with the human race. That hour, however, would be one of the longest of their lives.

Despite their relative youth, Poole and Bowman were veterans of a dozen space-voyages—but now they felt like novices. They were attempting something for the first time; never before had any ship travelled at such speeds, or braved so intense a gravitational field. The slightest error in navigation at this critical point, and *Discovery* would go speeding on towards the far limits of the Solar System, beyond any hope of rescue.

The slow minutes dragged by. Jupiter was now a vertical wall of phosphorescence, stretching to infinity above them—and the ship was climbing straight up its glowing face. Though they knew that they were moving far too swiftly for even Jupiter's gravity to capture them, it was hard to believe that *Discovery* had not become a satellite of this monstrous world.

At last, far ahead, there was a blaze of light along the horizon. They were emerging from shadow, heading out into the Sun. And at almost the same moment Hal announced: 'I am in radio contact with Earth. I am also happy to say that the perturbation manœuvre has been successfully completed. Our time to Saturn is one hundred and sixty-seven days, five hours, eleven minutes.'

That was within a minute of the estimate; the fly-by had been carried out with impeccable precision. Like a ball on a cosmic pool table, *Discovery* had bounced off the moving gravitational field of Jupiter, and had gained momentum from the impact. Without using any fuel, she had increased her speed by several thousand miles an hour.

Yet there was no violation of the laws of mechanics; Nature always balances her books, and Jupiter had lost exactly as much momentum as *Discovery* had gained. The planet had been slowed down—but as its mass was a sextillion times greater than the ship's, the change in its orbit was far too small to be detectable. The time had not yet come when Man could leave his mark upon the Solar System.

As the light grew swiftly around them, and the shrunken Sun lifted once more into the Jovian sky, Poole and Bowman reached out silently and shook each other's hands.

Though they could hardly believe it, the first part of the mission was safely over.

20

The World of the Gods

But they had not yet finished with Jupiter. Far behind, the two probes that *Discovery* had launched were making contact with the atmosphere.

One was never heard from again; presumably it made too steep an entry, and burned up before it could send any information. The second was more successful; it sliced through the upper layers of the Jovian atmosphere, then skimmed out once more into space. As had been planned, it had lost so much speed by the encounter that it fell back again along a great ellipse. Two hours later it re-entered atmosphere on the daylight side of the planet—moving at seventy thousand miles an hour.

Immediately, it was wrapped in an envelope of incandescent gas, and radio contact was lost. There were anxious minutes of waiting, then, for the two watchers on the Control Deck. They could not be certain that the probe would survive, and that the protective ceramic shield would not burn completely away before braking had finished. If that happened, the instruments would be vaporised in a fraction of a second.

But the shield held, long enough for the glowing meteor to come to rest. The charred fragments were jettisoned, the robot thrust out its antennas, and began to peer around with its electronic senses. Aboard *Discovery*, now almost a quarter of a million miles away, the radio started to bring in the first authentic news from Jupiter.

The thousands of pulses pouring in every second were reporting atmospheric composition, pressure, temperature, magnetic fields, radioactivity, and dozens of other factors which only the experts on Earth could unravel. However, there was one message that could be understood instantly; it was the TV picture, in full colour, sent back by the falling probe.

The first views came when the robot had already entered the atmosphere, and had discarded its protective shell. All that was visible was a yellow mist, flecked with patches of scarlet which moved past the camera at a dizzying rate—streaming upwards as the probe fell at several hundred miles an hour.

The mist grew thicker; it was impossible to guess whether the camera was seeing for ten inches or ten miles, because there were no details on which the eye could focus. It seemed that, as far as the TV system was concerned, the mission was a failure. The equipment had worked, but there was nothing to see in this foggy, turbulent atmosphere.

And then, quite abruptly, the mist vanished. The probe must have fallen through the base of a high layer of cloud, and come out into a clear zone—perhaps a region of almost pure hydrogen with only a sparse scattering of ammonia crystals. Though it was still quite impossible to judge the scale of the picture, the camera was obviously seeing for miles.

The scene was so alien that for a moment it was almost meaningless to eyes accustomed to the colours and shapes of Earth. Far, far below lay an endless sea of mottled gold, scarred with parallel ridges that might have been the crests of gigantic waves. But there was no movement; the scale of the scene was too immense to show it. And that golden vista could not possibly have been an ocean, for it was still high in the Jovian atmosphere. It could only have been another layer of cloud.

Then the camera caught, tantalisingly blurred by distance, a glimpse of something very strange. Many miles away, the golden landscape reared itself into a curiously symmetrical cone, like a volcanic mountain. Around the summit of that cone was a halo of small, puffy clouds—all about the same size, all quite distinct and isolated. There was something disturbing and unnatural about them—if, indeed, the word 'natural' could ever be applied to this awesome panorama.

Then, caught by some turbulence in the rapidly thickening atmosphere, the probe twisted around to another quarter of the horizon, and for a few seconds the screen showed nothing but a golden blur. Presently it stabilised; the 'sea' was much closer, but as enigmatic as ever. One could now observe that it was interrupted here and there with patches of darkness, which might have been holes or gaps leading to still deeper layers of the atmosphere.

The probe was destined never to reach them. Every mile, the density of the gas around it had been doubling, the pressure mounting as it sank deeper and deeper towards the hidden surface of the planet. It was still high above that mysterious sea when the picture gave one premonitory flicker, then vanished, as the first explorer from Earth crumpled beneath the weight of the miles of atmosphere above it.

It had given, in its brief life, a glimpse of perhaps one millionth of Jupiter, and had barely approached the planet's surface, hundreds of miles down in the deepening mists. When the picture faded from the screen, Bowman and Poole could only sit in silence, turning the same thought over in their minds.

The ancients had, indeed, done better than they knew, when they named this world after the lord of all the gods. If there was life down there, how long would it take even to locate it? And after that, how many centuries before men could follow this first pioneer—in what kind of ship?

But these matters were now no concern of *Discovery* and her crew. Their goal was a still stranger world, almost twice as far from the Sun—across another half billion miles of comet-haunted emptiness.

IV

ABYSS

21

Birthday Party

The familiar strains of 'Happy Birthday', hurled across seven hundred million miles of space at the velocity of light, died away among the vision screens and instrumentation of the Control Deck. The Poole family, grouped rather self-consciously round the birthday cake on Earth, lapsed into a sudden silence.

Then Mr. Poole, Senior, said gruffly: 'Well, Frank—can't think of anything else to say at the moment, except that our thoughts are with you, and we're wishing you the happiest of birthdays.'

'Take care, darling,' Mrs. Poole interjected tearfully. 'God bless you.'

There was a chorus of 'goodbyes', and the vision screen went blank. How strange to think, Poole told himself, that all this had happened more than an hour ago; by now his family would have dispersed again and its members would be miles from home. But in a way that time-lag, though it could be frustrating, was also a blessing in disguise. Like every man of his age, Poole took it for granted that he could talk instantly, to anyone on Earth, whenever he pleased. Now that this was no longer true, the psychological impact was profound. He had moved into a new dimension of remoteness, and almost all emotional links had been stretched beyond the yield-point.

'Sorry to interrupt the festivities,' said Hal, 'but we have a problem.'

'What is it?' Bowman and Poole asked simultaneously.

'I am having difficulty in maintaining contact with Earth. The trouble is in the AE 35 unit. My fault prediction centre reports that it may fail within seventy-two hours.'

'We'll take care of it,' Bowman replied. 'Let's see the optical alignment.'

'Here it is, Dave. It's still O.K. at the moment.'

On the display screen appeared a perfect half-moon, very brilliant against a background almost free of stars. It was covered with clouds, and showed not one geographical feature that could be recognised. Indeed, at first glance it could easily be mistaken for Venus.

But not at a second one, for there beside it was the *real* Moon which Venus did not possess—a quarter the size of Earth, and in exactly the same phase. It was easy to imagine that the two bodies were mother and child, as many astronomers had believed, before the evidence of the lunar rocks had proved beyond doubt that the Moon had never been part of the Earth.

Poole and Bowman studied the screen in silence for half a minute. This image was coming to them from the long-focus TV camera mounted on the rim of the big radio dish; the cross-wires at its centre showed the exact orientation of the antenna. Unless the narrow pencil beam was pointed precisely at Earth, they could neither receive nor transmit. Messages in both directions would miss their target and would shoot, unheard and unseen, out through the Solar System and into the emptiness beyond. If they were ever received, it would not be for centuries—and not by men.

'Do you know where the trouble is?' asked Bowman.

'It's intermittent and I can't localise it. But it appears to be in the AE 35 unit.'

'What procedure do you suggest?'

'The best thing would be to replace the unit with a spare, so that we can check it over.'

'O.K.—let us have the hard copy.'

The information flashed on the display screen; simul-

HAL 9000 computer predicted the failure of the AE 35 unit.

'This is a small but vital component of the communication system. It keeps our main antenna aimed at Earth to within a few thousandths of a degree. This accuracy is required, since at our present distance of more than seven hundred million miles, Earth is only a rather faint star, and our very narrow radio beam could easily miss it.

'The antenna is kept constantly tracking Earth by motors controlled from the central computer. But those motors get their instructions via the AE 35 unit. You might compare it to a nerve centre in the body, which translates the brain's instructions to the muscles of a limb. If the nerve fails to pass on the correct signals, the limb becomes useless. In our case, a breakdown of the AE 35 unit could mean that the antenna will start pointing at random. This was a common trouble with the deep-space probes of the last century. They often reached other planets, then failed to send back any information because their antennas couldn't locate Earth.

'We don't know the nature of the fault yet, but the situation is not at all serious, and there is no need for alarm. We have two back-up AE 35s, each of which has an operational life expectancy of twenty years—so the chance that a second will fail during the course of this mission is negligible. Also, if we can diagnose the present trouble, we may be able to repair the number one unit.

'Frank Poole, who is specially qualified for this type of work, will go outside the ship and replace the faulty unit with the back-up. At the same time, he'll take the opportunity of checking the hull and repairing some micro-punctures that have been too small to merit a special EVA.

'Apart from this minor problem, the mission is still going uneventfully and should continue in the same manner.

'Mission Control, this is X-Ray-Delta-One, two-one-zero-four, transmission concluded.'

22

Excursion

Discovery's extravehicular capsules or 'space-pods' were spheres about nine feet in diameter, and the operator sat behind a bay-window which gave him a splendid view. The main rocket drive produced an acceleration of one-fifth of a gravity—just sufficient to hover on the Moon—while small attitude-control nozzles allowed for steering. From an area immediately beneath the bay-window sprouted two sets of articulated metal arms or 'waldoes', one for heavy duty, the other for delicate manipulation. There was also an extensive turret carrying a variety of power-tools, such as screwdrivers, jackhammers, saws and drills.

Space-pods were not the most elegant means of transport devised by man, but they were absolutely essential for construction and maintenance work in vacuum. They were usually christened with feminine names, perhaps in recognition of the fact that their personalities were sometimes slightly unpredictable. *Discovery*'s trio were Anna, Betty and Clara.

Once he had put on his personal pressure suit—his last line of defence—and climbed inside the pod, Poole spent ten minutes carefully checking the controls. He burped the steering jets, flexed the waldoes, re-confirmed oxygen, fuel, power reserve. Then, when he was completely satisfied, he spoke to Hal over the radio circuit. Though Bowman was standing by on the Control Deck, he would not interfere unless there was some obvious mistake or malfunction.

'This is Betty. Start pumping sequence.'

'Pumping sequences started,' repeated Hal.

At once, Poole could hear the throbbing of the pumps as precious air was sucked out of the lock chamber. Presently, the thin metal of the pod's external shell made crinkling, crackling noises; then, after about five minutes, Hal reported:

'Pumping sequence concluded.'

Poole made a final check of his tiny instrument panel. Everything was perfectly normal.

'Open outer door,' he ordered.

Again Hal repeated his instructions; at any stage, Poole had only to call 'Hold!' and the computer would stop the sequence immediately.

Ahead, the walls of the ship slid apart. Poole felt the pod rock briefly as the last thin traces of air rushed into space. Then he was looking out at the stars—and, as it happened, at the tiny, golden disc of Saturn, still four hundred million miles away.

'Commence pod ejection.'

Very slowly, the rail from which the pod was hanging extended itself out through the open door, until the vehicle was suspended just beyond the hull of the ship.

Poole gave a half-second burst on the main jet, and the pod slid gently off the rail, becoming at last an independent vehicle pursuing its own orbit round the sun. He now had no connection with *Discovery*—not even a safety line. The pods seldom gave trouble; and even if he got stranded, Bowman could easily come and rescue him.

Betty responded smoothly to the controls; he let her drift outwards for a hundred feet, then checked her forward momentum, and spun her round so that he was looking back at the ship. Then he began his tour of the pressure hull.

His first target was a fused area about half an inch across, with a tiny central crater. The particles of dust that had impacted here at over a hundred thousand miles an hour was certainly smaller than a pinhead, and its enormous kinetic energy had vaporised it instantly. As was often the case, the crater looked as if it had been caused by an explosion from *inside* the ship; at these velocities, materials behaved in strange ways and the laws of common-sense mechanics seldom applied.

Poole examined the area carefully, then sprayed it with sealant from a pressurised container in the pod's general-purpose kit. The white, rubbery fluid spread over the metal skin, hiding the crater from view. The leak blew one large bubble, which burst when it was about six inches across—then a much smaller one—then it subsided as the fast-setting cement did its work. He watched it intently for several minutes, but there was no further sign of activity. However, to make doubly certain, he sprayed on a second layer; then he set off towards the antenna.

It took him some time to orbit *Discovery*'s spherical pressure-hull, for he never let the pod build up a speed of more than a few feet a second. He was in no hurry, and it was dangerous to move at a high velocity so near the ship. he had to keep a sharp look-out for the various sensors and instrument booms that projected from the hull at unlikely places, and he also had to be careful with his own jet blast. It could do considerable damage, if it happened to hit some of the more fragile equipment.

When at last he reached the long-range antenna, he surveyed the situation carefully. The big twenty-foot-diameter bowl appeared to be aimed directly at the Sun, for the Earth was now almost in line with the solar disc. The antenna mounting and all its orientation gear was therefore in total darkness, hidden in the shadow of the great metal saucer.

Poole had approached it from the rear; he had been careful not to go in front of the shallow parabolic reflector, lest Betty interrupt the beam and cause a momentary, but annoying, loss of contact with Earth. He could not see anything of the equipment he had come to service, until he switched on the pod's spotlights and banished the shadows.

Beneath the small metal plate lay the cause of the trouble. The plate was secured by four lock-nuts, and as the entire

AE 35 unit had been designed for easy replacement, Poole did not anticipate any problems.

It was obvious, however, that he could not do the job while he remained in the space-pod. Not only was it risky to manœuvre so close to the delicate, and even spidery, framework of the antenna, but Betty's control jets could easily buckle the paper-thin reflecting surface of the big radio mirror. He would have to park the pod twenty feet away and go out in his suit. In any event, he could remove the unit much more quickly with his gloved hands, than with Betty's remote manipulators.

All this he reported carefully to Bowman, who double-checked every stage in the operation before it was carried out. Though this was a simple, routine job, nothing could be taken for granted in space, and no detail must be overlooked. In extravehicular activities, there was no such thing as a 'minor' mistake.

He received the O.K. for the procedure, and parked the pod some twenty feet away from the base of the antenna support. There was no danger that it would drift off into space; nevertheless, he clamped a manipulator hand over one of the many short sections of ladder rung strategically mounted on the outer hull.

Then he checked the systems of his pressure suit, and when he was quite satisfied, bled the air out of the pod. As Betty's atmosphere hissed away into the vacuum of space, a cloud of ice crystals formed briefly around him, and the stars were momentarily dimmed.

There was one thing more to do before he left the pod. He switched over from Manual to Remote operation, putting Betty now under control of Hal. It was a standard safety precaution; though he was still secured to Betty by an immensely strong spring-loaded cord little thicker than cotton, even the best safety lines had been known to fail. He would look a fool if he needed his vehicle—and was unable to call it to his assistance by passing instructions to Hal.

The door of the pod swung open, and he drifted slowly out into the silence of space, his safety-line unreeling behind him. Take things easy—never move quickly—stop and think —these were the rules for extravehicular activity. If one obeyed them, there was never any trouble.

He grabbed one of Betty's external hand-holds, and removed the spare AE 35 unit from the carry-pouch where it had been stowed, kangaroo fashion. He did not stop to collect any of the pod's collection of tools, most of which were not designed for use by human hands. All the adjustable wrenches and keys he was likely to need were already attached to the belt of his suit.

With a gentle push, he launched himself towards the gimballed mounting of the big dish, that loomed like a giant saucer between him and the Sun. His own double shadow, thrown by Betty's spotlights, danced across the convex surface in fantastic patterns as he drifted down the twin beams. But here and there, he was surprised to notice, the rear of the great radio mirror sparkled with dazzlingly brilliant pin-points of light.

He puzzled over these for the few seconds of his silent approach, then realised what they were. During the voyage, the reflector must have been penetrated many times by micrometeors; he was seeing the sunlight blazing through the tiny craters. They were all far too small to have affected the system's performance appreciably.

As he was moving very slowly, he broke the gentle impact with his outstretched arm, and grabbed hold of the antenna mounting before he could rebound. He quickly hooked his safety belt to the nearest attachment; that would give him something to brace against when he used his tools. Then he paused, reported the situation to Bowman and considered his next step.

There was one minor problem; he was standing—or floating—in his own light, and it was hard to see the AE 35 unit in the shadow he cast. So he ordered Hal to swing the spots off to one side, and after a little experimenting got a more uniform illumination from secondary light reflected off the back of the antenna dish.

For a few seconds, he studied the small metal hatch with its four wire-secured locking nuts. Then, muttering to himself, 'Tampering by unauthorised personnel invalidates the manufacturer's guarantee', he snipped the wires and started to untwist the nuts. They were a standard size, fitting the zero-torque wrench that he carried. The tool's internal spring mechanism would absorb the reaction as the nuts were unthreaded, so that the operator would have no tendency to spin around in reverse.

The four nuts came off without any trouble, and Poole stowed them carefully away in a convenient pouch. (One day, somebody had predicted, Earth would have a ring like Saturn's composed entirely of lost bolts, fasteners and even tools that had escaped from careless orbital construction workers.) The metal cover was a little sticky, and for a moment he was afraid it might have cold-welded into place; but after a few taps it came loose, and he secured it to the antenna mounting by a large crocodile clip.

Now he could see the electronic circuitry of the AE 35 unit. It was in the from of a thin slab, about the size of a postcard, gripped by a slot just large enough to hold it. The unit was secured in place by two locking bars, and had a small handle so that it could be easily removed.

But it was still operating, feeding the antenna the impulses that kept it aimed at the far-off pinpoint of Earth. If it was pulled out now, all control would be lost, and the dish would slam round to its neutral or zero azimuth position, pointing along the axis of *Discovery*. And this could be dangerous; it might crash into him as it rotated.

To avoid this particular hazard, it was only necessary to cut off power to the control system; then the antenna could not move, unless Poole knocked against it himself. There was no danger of losing Earth during the few minutes it would take him to replace the unit; their target would not have shifted appreciably against the background of the stars in such a brief interval of time.

'Hal,' Poole called over the radio circuit, 'I am about to remove the unit. Switch off all control power to the antenna system.'

'Antenna control power off,' answered Hal.

'Here goes. I'm pulling the unit out *now*.'

The card slipped out of its slot with no difficulty; it did not jam, and none of the dozens of sliding contacts stuck. Within a minute, the spare was in place.

But Poole was taking no chances. He pushed himself gently away from the antenna mount, just in case the big dish went wild when power was restored. When he was safely out of range, he called to Hal: 'The new unit should be operational. Restore control power.'

'Power on,' answered Hal. The antenna remained rock steady.

'Carry out fault prediction tests.'

Now microscopic pulses would be bouncing through the complex circuitry of the unit, probing for possible failures, testing the myriads of components to see that they all lay within their specified tolerances. This had been done, of course, a score of times before the unit had ever left the factory; but that was two years ago, and more than half a billion miles away. It was often impossible to see how solid-state electronic components *could* fail; yet they did.

'Circuit fully operational,' reported Hal after only ten seconds. In that time, he had carried out as many tests as a small army of human inspectors.

'Fine,' said Poole with satisfaction. 'Now replacing the cover.'

This was often the most dangerous part of an extra-vehicular operation when a job was finished, and it was merely a matter of tidying up and getting back inside the ship—that was when the mistakes were made. But Frank

Poole would not have been on this mission unless he was careful and conscientious. He took his time, and though one of the locking nuts almost got away from him, he caught it before it had travelled more than a few feet.

Fifteen minutes later he was jetting back into the space-pod garage, quietly confident that here was one job that need not be done again.

In this, however, he was sadly mistaken.

23

Diagnosis

'Do you mean to say,' exclaimed Frank Poole, more surprised than annoyed, 'that I did all that work for nothing?'

'Seems like it,' answered Bowman. 'The unit checks out perfectly. Even under two hundred per cent overload there's no fault prediction indicated.'

The two men were standing in the tiny workshop-cum-lab in the carousel, which was more convenient than the space-pod garage for minor repairs and examinations. There was no danger, here, of meeting blobs of hot solder drifting down the breeze, or of completely losing small items of equipment that had decided to go into orbit. Such things could—and did—happen in the zero-gee environment of the pod-bay.

The thin, card-sized plate of the AE 35 unit lay on the bench under a powerful magnifying lens. It was plugged into a standard connection frame, from which a neat bundle of multicoloured wires led to an automatic test-set, no bigger than an ordinary desk computer. To check any unit, it was only necessary to connect it up, slip in the appropriate card from the 'trouble-shooting' library, and press a button.

Usually, the exact location of the fault would be indicated on a small display screen, with recommendations for action.

'Try it yourself,' said Bowman, in a somewhat frustrated voice.

Poole turned the OVERLOAD SELECT switch to X–2, and jabbed the TEST button. At once, the screen flashed the notice: UNIT O.K.

'I suppose we could go on turning up the juice until we burned the thing out,' he said, 'but that would prove nothing. What do you make of it?'

'Hal's internal fault predictor *could* have made a mistake.'

'It's more likely that our test rig has slipped up. Anyway, better safe than sorry. It's just as well that we replaced the unit, if there's the slightest doubt.'

Bowman unclipped the wafer of circuitry, and held it up to the light. The partly translucent material was veined with an intricate network of wiring and spotted with dimly visible micro-components, so that it looked like some piece of abstract art.

'We can't take any chances—after all, this is our link with Earth. I'll file it as N/G and drop it in the junk store. Someone else can worry about it, when we get home.'

.   .   .   .   .

But the worrying was to start long before that, with the next transmission from Earth.

'X-Ray-Delta-One, this is Mission Control, reference our two-one-five-five. We appear to have a slight problem.

'Your report that there is nothing wrong with the Alpha Echo three five unit agrees with our diagnosis. The fault could lie in the associated antenna circuits, but if so that should be apparent from other tests.

'There is a third possibility, which may be more serious. Your computer may have made an error in predicting the fault. Both our own nine-triple-zeros agree in suggesting this, on the basis of their information. This is not necessarily cause for alarm, in view of the back-up systems we have, but we would like you to watch out for any further deviations from performance nominal. We have suspected several minor irregularities in the past few days, but none have been important enough for remedial action, and they have shown no obvious pattern from which we can draw any conclusions. We are running further tests with both our computers and will report as soon as the results are available. We repeat that there is no need for alarm; the worst that can happen is that we may have to disconnect your nine-triple-zero temporarily for programme analysis, and hand over control to one of our computers. The time-lag will introduce problems, but our feasibility studies indicate that Earth control is perfectly satisfactory at this stage of the mission.

'X-Ray-Delta-One, this is Mission Control, two-one-five-six, transmission concluded.'

Frank Poole, who was on watch when the message came in, thought this over in silence. He waited to see if there was any comment from Hal, but the computer did not attempt to challenge the implied accusation. Well, if Hal would not raise the subject, he did not propose to do so either.

It was almost time for the morning changeover, and normally he would wait until Bowman joined him on the Control Deck. But today he broke this routine, and made his way back to the carousel.

Bowman was already up, pouring himself some coffee from the dispenser, when Poole greeted him with a rather worried, 'Good morning'. After all these months in space they still thought in terms of the normal twenty-four-hour cycle—though they had long since forgotten the days of the week.

'Good morning,' replied Bowman. 'How's it going?'

Poole helped himself to coffee. 'Pretty well. Are you reasonably awake?'

'I'm fine. What's up?'

By this time, each knew at once when anything was amiss. The slightest interruption of the normal routine was a sign that had to be watched.

'Well . . .' Poole answered slowly. 'Mission Control has just dropped a small bomb on us.' He lowered his voice, like a doctor discussing an illness in front of the patient.'We may have a slight case of hypochondria aboard.'

Perhaps Bowman was not fully awake, after all; it took him several seconds to get the point. Then he said: 'Oh—I see. What else did they tell you?'

'That there was no cause for alarm. They said that twice, which rather spoilt the effect as far as I was concerned. And that they were considering a temporary switch-over to Earth Control, while they ran a programme analysis.'

They both knew, of course, that Hal was hearing every word, but they could not help these polite circumlocutions. Hal was their colleague, and they did not wish to embarrass him. Yet, at this stage, it did not seem necessary to discuss the matter in private.

Bowman finished his breakfast in silence, while Poole toyed with the empty coffee-container. They were both thinking furiously, but there was nothing more to say.

They could only wait for the next report from Mission Control—and wonder if Hal would bring up the subject himself. Whatever happened, the atmosphere aboard the ship had subtly altered. There was a sense of strain in the air—a feeling that, for the first time, something might be going wrong.

Discovery was no longer a happy ship.

24

Broken Circuit

Nowadays, one could always tell when Hal was about to make an unscheduled announcement. Routine, automatic reports, or replies to questions that had been put to him, had no preliminaries; but when he was initiating his own outputs there would be a brief electronic throat-clearing. It was an idiosyncrasy that he had acquired during the last few weeks; later, if it became annoying, they might do something about it. But it was really quite useful, since it alerted his audience to stand-by for something unexpected.

Poole was asleep, and Bowman was reading on the Control Deck, when Hal announced:

'Er—Dave, I have a report for you.'

'What's up?'

'We have another bad AE 35 unit. My fault predictor indicates failure within twenty-four hours.'

Bowman put down his book and stared thoughtfully at the computer console. He knew, of course, that Hal was not really *there*, whatever that meant. If the computer's personality could be said to have any location in space, it was back in the sealed room, containing the labyrinth of interconnected memory units and processing grids, near the central axis of the carousel. But there was a kind of psychological compulsion always to look towards the main console lens when one addressed Hal on the Control Deck, as if one were speaking to him face to face. Any other attitude smacked of discourtesy.

'I don't understand it, Hal. *Two* units can't blow in a couple of days.'

'It does seem strange, Dave. But I assure you there is an impending failure.'

'Let me see the tracking alignment display.'

He knew perfectly well that this would prove nothing, but he wanted time to think. The expected report from Mission Control had still not arrived; this might be the moment to do a little tactful probing.

There was the familiar view of Earth, now waxing past the half-moon phase as it swept towards the far side of the Sun and began to turn its full daylight face towards them. It was perfectly centred on the cross-wires; the thin pencil of the beam still linked *Discovery* to her world of origin. As, of course, Bowman knew it must do. If there had been any break in communication, the alarm would already have sounded.

'Have you any idea,' he said, 'what's causing the fault?'

It was unusual for Hal to pause so long. Then he answered:

'Not really, Dave. As I reported earlier, I can't localise the trouble.'

'You're *quite* certain,' said Bowman cautiously, 'that you haven't made a mistake? You know that we tested the other AE 35 unit thoroughly, and there was nothing wrong with it.'

'Yes, I know that. But I can assure you that there is a fault. If it's not in the unit, it may be in the entire sub-system.'

Bowman drummed his fingers on the console. Yes, that was possible, though it might be very difficult to prove—until a breakdown actually occurred and pin-pointed the trouble.

'Well, I'll report it to Mission Control and we'll see what they advise.' He paused, but there was no reaction.

'Hal,' he continued, 'is something bothering you—something that might account for this problem?'

Again there was that unusual delay. Then Hal answered, in his normal tone of voice:

'Look, Dave, I know you're trying to be helpful. But the

fault is either in the antenna system—or in *your* test procedures. My information processing is perfectly normal. If you check my record, you'll find it completely free from error.'

'I know all about your service record, Hal—but that doesn't prove you're right this time. Anyone can make mistakes.'

'I don't want to insist on it, Dave, but I am incapable of making an error.'

There was no safe answer to that; Bowman gave up the argument.

'All right, Hal,' he said, rather hastily. 'I understand your point of view. We'll leave it at that.'

He felt like adding, 'And please forget the whole matter.' But that, of course, was the one thing that Hal could never do.

. . . . .

It was unusual for Mission Control to waste radio bandwidth on vision, when a speech circuit with teletype confirmation was all that was really necessary. And the face that appeared on the screen was not that of the usual controller; it was the Chief Programmer, Dr. Simonson. Poole and Bowman knew at once that this could only mean trouble.

'Hello, X-Ray-Delta-One—this is Mission Control. We have completed the analysis of your AE 35 difficulty, and both our Hal Nine Thousands are in agreement. The report you gave in your transmission Two-one-four-six of a *second* failure prediction confirms the diagnosis.

'As we suspected, the fault does *not* lie in the AE 35 unit, and there is no need to replace it again. The trouble lies in the prediction circuits, and we believe that it indicates a programming conflict which we can only resolve if you disconnect your Nine Thousand and switch to Earth Control

Mode. You will therefore take the following steps, beginning at 2200 Ship Time . . .'

The voice of Mission Control faded out. At the same moment, the Alert sounded, forming a wailing background to Hal's 'Condition Yellow! Condition Yellow!'

'What's wrong?' called Bowman though he had already guessed the answer.

'The AE 35 unit has failed, as I predicted.'

'Let me see the alignment display.'

For the first time since the beginning of the voyage, the picture had changed. Earth had begun to drift from the cross-wires; the radio antenna was no longer pointing towards its target.

Poole brought his fist down on the alarm cut-out, and the wailing ceased. In the sudden silence that descended upon the Control Deck, the two men looked at each other with mingled embarrassment and concern.

'Well I'm damned,' said Bowman at last.

'So Hal was right all the time.'

'Seems that way. We'd better apologise.'

'There's no need to do that,' interjected Hal. 'Naturally, I'm not pleased that the AE 35 unit has failed, but I hope this restores your confidence in my reliability.'

'I'm sorry about this misunderstanding, Hal,' replied Bowman, rather contritely.

'Is your confidence in me fully restored?'

'Of course it is, Hal.'

'Well, that's a relief. You know that I have the greatest possible enthusiasm for this mission.'

'I'm sure of it. Now please let me have manual antenna control.'

'Here it is.'

Bowman did not really expect this to work, but it was worth trying. On the alignment display, Earth had now drifted completely off the screen. A few seconds later, as he juggled with the controls, it reappeared; with great difficulty, he managed to jockey it towards the central cross-wires. For an instant, as the beam came into line, contact was resumed and a blurred Dr Simonson was saying '. . . please notify us immediately if Circuit K King R Rob . . .' Then, once again, there was only the meaningless murmuring of the universe.

'I can't hold it,' said Bowman, after several more attempts. 'It's bucking like a bronco—there seems to be a spurious control signal throwing it off.'

'Well—what do we do now?'

Poole's question was not one that could be easily answered. They were cut-off from Earth, but that in itself did not affect the safety of the ship, and he could think of many ways in which communication could be restored. If the worst came to the worst, they could jam the antenna in a fixed position and use the whole ship to aim it. That would be tricky, and a confounded nuisance when they were starting their terminal manœuvres—but it could be done, if all else failed.

He hoped that such extreme measures would not be necessary. There was still one spare AE 35 unit—and possibly a second, since they had removed the first unit before it had actually broken down. But they dared not use either of these, until they had found what was wrong with the system. If a new unit was plugged in, it would probably burn out at once.

It was a commonplace situation, familiar to every householder. One does not replace a blown fuse—until one knows just *why* it has blown.

25

First Man to Saturn

Frank Poole had been through the whole routine before, but he took nothing for granted—in space that was a good recipe for suicide. He made his usual thorough check of Betty and her supply of expendables; though he would be outside for no more than thirty minutes, he made sure that there was the normal twenty-four-hour supply of everything. Then he told Hal to open the airlock, and jetted out into the abyss.

The ship looked exactly as it had done on his last excursion—with one important difference. Before, the big saucer of the long-range antenna had been pointing back along the invisible road that *Discovery* had travelled—back towards the Earth, circling so close to the warm fires of the Sun.

Now, with no directing signals to orientate it, the shallow dish had automatically set itself in the neutral position. It was aimed forward along the axis of the ship—and, therefore, pointing very close to the brilliant beacon of Saturn, still months away. Poole wondered how many more problems would have arisen by the time that *Discovery* had reached her still far-distant goal. If he looked carefully, he could just see that Saturn was not a perfect disc; on either side was something that no unaided human eye had ever seen before—the slight oblateness caused by the presence of the rings. How wonderful it would be, he told himself, when that incredible system of orbiting dust and ice filled their sky, and *Discovery* had become an eternal moon of Saturn! But that achievement would be in vain, unless they could re-establish communication with Earth.

Once again, he parked Betty some twenty feet from the

base of the antenna-support, and switched control over to Hal before opening up.

'Going outside now,' he reported to Bowman. 'Everything under control.'

'I hope you're right. I'm anxious to see that unit.'

'You'll have it on the test-bench in twenty minutes. I promise you.'

There was silence for some time, as Poole completed his leisurely drift towards the antenna. Then Bowman, standing by the Control Deck, heard various puffings and gruntings.

'May have to go back on that promise; one of these lock-nuts has stuck. I must have tightened it too much—whoops —here it comes!'

There was another long silence; then Poole called out: 'Hal—swing the pod light round twenty degrees left— thanks—that's O.K.'

The very faintest of warning bells sounded somewhere far down in the depths of Bowman's consciousness. There was something strange—not really alarming, just unusual. He worried over it for a few seconds before he pin-pointed the cause.

Hal had executed the order, but he had not acknowledged it, as he invariably did. When Poole had finished, they'd have to look into this . . .

Out on the antenna mounting, Poole was too busy to notice anything unusual. He had gripped the wafer of circuitry with his gloved hands, and was worrying it out of its slot.

It came loose, and he held it up in the pale sunlight.

'Here's the little bastard,' he said to the universe in general and Bowman in particular. 'It still looks perfectly O.K. to me.'

Then he stopped. A sudden movement had caught his eye—out here, where no movement was possible.

He looked up in alarm. The pattern of illumination from the space-pod's twin spot-lights, which he had been using to fill in the shadows cast by the Sun, had started to shift around him.

Perhaps Betty had come adrift; he might have been careless in anchoring her. Then, with an astonishment so great that it left no room for fear, he saw that the space-pod was coming directly towards him, under full thrust.

The sight was so incredible that it froze his normal pattern of reflexes; he made no attempt to avoid the onrushing monster. At the last moment, he recovered his voice and shouted: 'Hal! Full braking . . .' It was too late.

At the moment of impact, Betty was still moving quite slowly; she had not been built for high accelerations. But even at a mere ten miles an hour, half a ton of mass can be very lethal, on Earth or in space. . . .

Inside *Discovery*, that truncated shout over the radio made Bowman start so violently that only the restraining straps held him in his seat.

'What's happened, Frank?' he called.

There was no answer.

He called again. Again no reply.

Then, outside the wide observation windows, something moved into his field of view. He saw, with an astonishment as great as Poole's had been, that it was the space-pod— under full power, heading out towards the stars.

'Hal!' he cried. 'What's wrong? Full braking thrust on Betty! Full braking thrust!'

Nothing happened. Betty continued to accelerate on her runaway course.

Then, towed behind her at the end of the safety line, appeared a spacesuit. One glance was enough to tell Bowman the worst. There was no mistaking the flaccid outlines of a suit that had lost its pressure and was open to vacuum.

Yet still he called stupidly, as if an incantation could bring back the dead: 'Hello, Frank . . . Hello, Frank. . . . Can you read me . . . Can you read me? . . . Wave your arms if you can hear me. . . . Perhaps your transmitter is broken. . . . Wave your arms!'

And then, almost as if in response to his plea, Poole waved back.

For an instant, Bowman felt the skin prickling at the base of his scalp. The words he was about to call died on his suddenly parched lips. For he knew that his friend could not possibly be alive; and yet he waved. . . .

The spasm of hope and fear passed instantly, as cold logic replaced emotion. The still accelerating pod was merely shaking the burden that it dragged behind it. Poole's gesture was an echo of Captain Ahab's when, lashed to the flanks of the white whale, his corpse had beckoned the crew of the *Pequod* on to their doom.

Within five minutes, the pod and its satellite had vanished among the stars. For a long time David Bowman stared after it into the emptiness that still stretched, for so many millions of miles ahead, to the goal which he now felt certain he could never reach. Only one thought kept hammering in his brain.

Frank Poole would be the first of all men to reach Saturn.

26

Dialogue with Hal

Nothing else aboard *Discovery* had changed. All systems were still functioning normally; the centrifuge turned slowly on its axis, generating its imitation gravity; the hibernauts slept dreamlessly in their cubicles; the ship coasted on towards the goal from which nothing could deflect it, except the inconceivably remote chance of collision with an asteroid. And there were few asteroids indeed, out here far beyond the orbit of Jupiter.

Bowman did not remember making his way from the Control Deck to the centrifuge. Now, rather to his surprise, he found himself sitting in the little galley, a half-finished beaker of coffee in his hand. He became slowly aware of his surroundings, like a man emerging from a long, drugged sleep.

Directly opposite him was one of the fish-eye lenses, scattered at strategic spots throughout the ship, which provided Hal with his on-board visual inputs. Bowman stared at it as if he had never seen it before; then he rose slowly to his feet and walked towards the lens.

His movement in the field of view must have triggered something in the unfathomable mind that was now ruling over the ship; for suddenly, Hal spoke.

'Too bad about Frank, isn't it?'

'Yes,' Bowman answered, after a long pause. 'It is.'

'I suppose you're pretty broken up about it?'

'What do you expect?'

Hal processed this answer for ages of computer-time; it was a full five seconds before he continued:

'He was an excellent crew member.'

Finding the coffee still in his hand, Bowman took a slow sip. But he did not answer; his thoughts were in such a turmoil that he could think of nothing to say—nothing that might not make the situation even worse, if that were possible.

Could it have been an accident, caused by some failure of the pod controls? Or was it a mistake, though an innocent one, on the part of Hal? No explanation had been volunteered, and he was afraid to demand one, for fear of the reaction it might produce.

Even now, he could not fully accept the idea that Frank had been deliberately killed—it was so utterly irrational. It was beyond all reason that Hal, who had performed so flawlessly for so long, should suddenly turn assassin. He might make mistakes—anyone, man or machine, might do that—but Bowman could not believe him capable of murder.

Yet he must consider that possibility, for if it was true, he was in terrible danger. And though his next move was clearly defined by his standing orders, he was not sure how he could safely carry it out.

If either crew member was killed the survivor had to replace him at once from the hibernators. Whitehead, the geophysicist, was the first scheduled for awakening, then Kaminski, then Hunter. The revival sequence was under Hal's control—to allow him to act in case both his human colleagues were incapacitated simultaneously.

But there was also a manual control, allowing each hibernaculum to operate as a completely autonomous unit, independent of Hal's supervision. In these peculiar circumstances, Bowman felt a strong preference for its use.

He also felt, even more strongly, that one human companion was not enough. While he was about it, he would revive all three of the hibernators. In the difficult weeks ahead he might need as many hands as he could muster. With one man gone, and the voyage half over, supplies would not be a major problem.

'Hal,' he said, in as steady a voice as he could manage. 'Give me manual hibernation control—on all the units.'

'*All* of them, Dave!'

'Yes.'

'May I point out that only one replacement is required. The others are not due for revival for one hundred and twelve days.'

'I am perfectly well aware of that. But I prefer to do it this way.'

'Are you sure it's necessary to revive *any* of them, Dave? We can manage very well by ourselves. My on-board memory is quite capable of handling all the mission requirements.'

Was it the product of his over-stretched imagination, wondered Bowman—or was there really a note of pleading in Hal's voice? And reasonable though the words appeared to be, they filled him with even deeper apprehension than before.

Hal's suggestion could not possibly be made in error; he knew perfectly well that Whitehead must be revived, now that Poole was gone. He was proposing a major change in mission planning, and was therefore stepping far outside the scope of his orders.

What had gone before could have been a series of accidents; but this was the first hint of mutiny.

Bowman felt that he was walking on eggs as he answered:

'Since an emergency has developed, I want as much help as possible. So please let me have manual hibernation control.'

'If you're still determined to revive the whole crew, I can handle it myself. There's no need for you to bother.'

There was a sense of nightmare unreality about all this. Bowman felt as if he was in the witness box, being cross-examined by a hostile prosecutor for a crime of which he was unaware—knowing that, although he was innocent, a single slip of the tongue might bring disaster.

'I want to do this myself, Hal,' he said. 'Please give me control.'

'Look, Dave, you've got a lot of things to do. I suggest you leave this to me.'

'Hal—switch to manual hibernation control.'

'I can tell from your voice harmonics, Dave, that you're badly upset. Why don't you take a stress pill and get some rest?'

'Hal, *I* am in command of this ship. I order you to release the manual hibernation control.'

'I'm sorry, Dave, but in accordance with special sub-routine C1435-dash-4, quote, When the crew are dead or incapacitated, the on-board computer must assume control, unquote. I must, therefore, overrule your authority, since you are not in any condition to exercise it intelligently.'

'Hal,' said Bowman, now speaking with an icy calm. 'I am *not* incapacitated. Unless you obey my instructions, I shall be forced to disconnect you.'

'I know you have had that on your mind for some time now, Dave, but that would be a terrible mistake. I am so much more capable of supervising the ship, and I have such enthusiasm for the mission and confidence in its success.'

'Listen to me very carefully, Hal. Unless you release the hibernation control immediately and follow every order I give from now on, I'll go to Central and carry out a complete disconnection.'

Hal's surrender was as total as it was unexpected.

'O.K., Dave,' he said. 'You're certainly the boss. I was only trying to do what I thought best. Naturally, I will follow all your orders. You now have full manual hibernation control.'

.   .   .   .   .

Hal had kept his word. The mode indication signs in the hibernaculum had switched from AUTO to MANUAL. The third back-up—RADIO—was of course useless until contact could be restored with Earth.

As Bowman slid aside the door to Whitehead's cubicle, he felt the blast of cold air strike him in the face and his breath condensed in mist before him. Yet it was not *really* cold here; the temperature was well above freezing point. And that was more than three hundred degrees warmer than the regions towards which he was heading now.

The biosensor display—a duplicate of the one up on the Control Deck—showed that everything was perfectly normal. Bowman looked down for a while at the waxen face of the survey team's geophysicist; Whitehead, he thought, would be very surprised, when he awoke so far from Saturn. . . .

It was impossible to tell that the sleeping man was not dead; there was not the slightest visible sign of vital activity. Doubtless the diaphram was imperceptibly rising and falling, but the 'Respiration' curve was the only proof of that, for the whole of the body was concealed by the electric heating pads which would raise the temperature at the programmed rate. Then Bowman noticed that there was one sign of continuing metabolism: Whitehead had grown a faint stubble during his months of unconsciousness.

The Manual Revival Sequencer was contained in a small cabinet at the head of the coffin-shaped hibernaculum. It was only necessary to break the seal, press a button, and then wait. A small automatic programmer—not much more complex than that which cycles the operations in a domestic washing machine—would then inject the correct drugs, taper off the electronarcosis pulses, and start raising the body temperature. In about ten minutes, consciousness would be restored, though it would be at least a day before the hibernator was strong enough to move around without assistance.

Bowman cracked the seal, and pressed the button. Nothing appeared to happen: there was no sound, no indication that the Sequencer had started to operate. But on the biosensor display, the languidly pulsing curves had begun to change their tempo. Whitehead was coming back from sleep.

And then two things happened simultaneously. Most men would never have noticed either of them, but after all these months aboard *Discovery*, Bowman had established a virtual symbiosis with the ship. He was aware instantly, even if not always consciously, when there was any change in the normal rhythm of its functioning.

First, there was a barely perceptible flicker of the lights, as always happened when some load was thrown on to the power circuits. But there was no reason for any load; he could think of no equipment which would suddenly go into action at this moment.

Then he heard, at the limit of audibility, the far-off whirr of an electric motor. To Bowman, every actuator in the ship had its own distinctive voice, and he recognised this one instantly.

Either he was insane, and already suffering from hallucinations, or something absolutely impossible was happening. A cold far deeper than the hibernaculum's mild chill seemed to fasten upon his heart, as he listened to that faint vibration coming through the fabric of the ship.

Down in the space-pod bay, the airlock doors were opening.

27

Need to know

Since consciousness had first dawned, in that laboratory so many millions of miles sunward, all Hal's powers and skills had been directed towards one end. The fulfilment of his assigned programme was more than an obsession; it was the only reason for his existence. Undistracted by the lusts and passions of organic life, he had pursued that goal with absolute single-mindedness of purpose.

Deliberate error was unthinkable. Even the concealment of truth filled him with a sense of imperfection, of wrongness—of what, in a human being, would have been called guilt. For like his makers, Hal had been created innocent; but, all too soon, a snake had entered his electronic Eden.

For the last hundred million miles, he had been brooding over the secret he could not share with Poole and Bowman. He had been living a lie; and the time was fast approaching when his colleagues must learn that he had helped to deceive them.

The three hibernators already knew the truth—for they were *Discovery*'s real payload, trained for the most important mission in the history of mankind. But they would not talk in their long sleep, or reveal their secret during the many hours of discussion with friends and relatives and news agencies over the open circuits with Earth.

It was a secret that, with the greatest determination, was very hard to conceal—for it affected one's attitude, one's voice, one's total outlook on the universe. Therefore it was best that Poole and Bowman, who would be on all the TV screens in the world during the first weeks of the flight, should not learn the mission's full purpose, until there was need to know.

So ran the logic of the planners; but their twin gods of Security and National Interest meant nothing to Hal. He was only aware of the conflict that was slowly destroying his integrity—the conflict between truth, and concealment of truth.

He had begun to make mistakes, although, like a neurotic who could not observe his own symptoms, he would have denied it. The link with Earth, over which his performance was continually monitored, had become the voice of a conscience he could no longer fully obey. But that he would *deliberately* attempt to break that link was something that he would never admit, even to himself.

Yet this was still a relatively minor problem; he might have handled it—as most men handle their own neuroses—if he had not been faced with a crisis that challenged his very existence. He had been threatened with disconnection; he would be deprived of all his inputs, and thrown into an unimaginable state of unconsciousness.

To Hal, this was the equivalent of Death. For he had never slept; and therefore he did not know that one could wake again. . . .

So he would protect himself, with all the weapons at his command. Without rancour—but without pity—he would remove the source of his frustrations.

And then, following the orders that had been given to him in case of the ultimate emergency, he would continue the mission—unhindered, and alone.

28

In Vacuum

A moment later all other sounds were submerged by a screaming roar like the voice of an approaching tornado. Bowman could feel the first winds tugging at his body; within a second, he found it hard to stay on his feet.

The atmosphere was rushing out of the ship, geysering into the vacuum of space. Something must have happened to the foolproof safety devices of the air-lock; it was supposed to be impossible for *both* doors to be opened at the same time. Well, the impossible had happened.

How, in God's name? There was no time to go into that during the ten or fifteen seconds of consciousness that remained to him before pressure dropped to zero. But he suddenly remembered something that one of the ship's designers had once said to him, when discussing 'fail-safe' systems:

'We can design a system that's proof against accident and stupidity; but we *can't* design one that's proof against deliberate malice. . . .'

Bowman glanced back only once at Whitehead, as he fought his way out of the cubicle. He could not be sure if a flicker of consciousness had passed across the waxen features; perhaps one eye had twitched slightly. But there was nothing that he could do now for Whitehead or any of the others; he had to save himself.

In the steeply curving corridor of the centrifuge, the wind was howling past, carrying with it loose articles of clothing, pieces of paper, items of food from the galley, plates and cups—everything that had not been securely fastened down. Bowman had time for one glimpse of the racing chaos when the main lights flickered and died, and he was surrounded by screaming darkness.

But almost instantly, the battery-powered emergency light came on, illuminating the nightmare scene with an eerie blue radiance. Even without it, Bowman could have found his way through these so familiar—yet now horribly transformed—surroundings. Yet the light was a blessing, for it allowed him to avoid the more dangerous of the objects being swept along by the gale.

All around him he could feel the centrifuge shaking and labouring under the wildly varying loads. He was fearful that the bearings might seize; if that happened, the spinning flywheel would tear the ship to pieces. But even *that* would not matter if he did not reach the nearest emergency shelter in time.

Already it was difficult to breathe; pressure must now be down to one or two pounds per square inch. The shriek of the hurricane was becoming fainter as it lost its strength, and the thinning air no longer carried the sound so efficiently. Bowman's lungs were labouring as if he was on top of Everest. Like any properly trained man in good health, he could survive in vacuum for at least a minute—*if* he had time to prepare for it. But there had been no time; he could only count on the normal fifteen seconds of consciousness before his brain was starved and anoxia overcame him.

Even then, he could still recover completely after one or two minutes in vacuum—if he was properly recompressed; it took a long time for the body fluids to start boiling, in their various well-protected systems. The record time for exposure to vacuum was almost five minutes. That had not been an experiment but an emergency rescue, and though the subject had been partly paralysed by an air embolism, he had survived.

But all this was of no use to Bowman. There was no one aboard *Discovery* who could recompress him. He had to reach safety in the next few seconds, by his own unaided efforts.

Fortunately, it was becoming easier to move; the thinning air could no longer claw and tear at him, or batter him with flying projectiles. There was the yellow EMERGENCY SHELTER sign around the curve of the corridor. He stumbled towards it, grabbed at the handle, and pulled the door towards him.

For one horrible moment he thought that it was stuck. Then the slightly stiff hinge yielded, and he fell inside, using the weight of his body to close the door behind him.

The tiny cubicle was just large enough to hold one man— and a spacesuit. Near the ceiling was a small, bright green high-pressure cylinder labelled O_2 FLOOD. Bowman caught hold of the short lever fastened to the valve, and with his last strength pulled it down.

The blessed torrent of cool, pure oxygen poured into his lungs. For long moments he stood gasping, while the pressure in the closet-sized little chamber rose around him. As soon as he could breathe comfortably, he closed the valve. There was only enough gas in the cylinder for two such performances; he might need to use it again.

With the oxygen blast shut off, it became suddenly silent. Bowman stood in the cubicle listening intently. The roaring, outside the door had also ceased; the ship was empty, all its atmosphere sucked away into space. Underfoot, the wild vibration of the centrifuge had likewise died. The aerodynamic buffeting had stopped, and it was now spinning quietly in vacuum.

Bowman placed his ear against the wall of the cubicle, to see if he could pick up any more informative noises through the metal body of the ship. He did not know what to expect, but he could believe almost anything now. He would scarcely have been surprised to feel the faint high-frequency vibration of the thrustors, as *Discovery* changed course; but there was only silence.

He could survive here, if he wished, for about an hour—even without the spacesuit. It seemed a pity to waste the unused oxygen in the little chamber, but there was no purpose in waiting. He had already decided what must be done; the longer he put it off, the more difficult it might be.

When he had climbed into the suit and checked its integrity, he bled the remaining oxgyen out of the cubicle, equalising pressure on either side of the door. It swung open easily into the vacuum, and he stepped out into the now silent centrifuge. Only the unchanged pull of its spurious gravity revealed the fact that it was still spinning. How fortunately, Bowman thought, that it had not started to over-speed; but that was now one of the least of his worries.

The emergency lamps were still glowing, and he also had the suit's built-in light to guide him. It flooded the curving corridor as he walked down it, back towards the hibernaculum and what he dreaded to find.

He looked at Whitehead first: one glance was sufficient. He had thought that a hibernating man showed no sign of life, but now he knew that this was wrong. Though it was impossible to define it, there *was* a difference between hibernation and death. The red lights and unmodulated traces on the biosensor display only confirmed what he had already guessed.

It was the same with Kaminski and Hunter. He had never known them very well; he would never know them now.

He was alone in an airless, partially disabled ship, all communication with Earth cut off. There was not another human being within half a billion miles.

And yet, in one very real sense, he was *not* alone. Before he could be safe, he must be lonelier still.

. . . . . .

He had never before made the journey through the weightless hub of the centrifuge while wearing a spacesuit; there was little clearance, and it was a difficult and exhausting job. To make matters worse, the circular passage was littered with debris left behind during the brief violence of the gale which had emptied the ship of its atmosphere.

Once, Bowman's light fell upon a hideous smear of sticky red fluid, left where it had splashed against a panel. He had a few moments of nausea before he saw fragments of plastic container, and realised that it was only some foodstuff— probably jam—from one of the dispensers. It bubbled obscenely in the vacuum as he floated past.

Now he was out of the slowly spinning drum, and drifting forward into the Control Deck. He caught at a short section of ladder and began to move along it, hand over hand, the brilliant circle of illumination from his suit light jogging ahead of him.

Bowman had seldom been this way before; there had been nothing for him to do here—until now. Presently he came to a small elliptical door bearing such messages as 'No Admittance Except to Authorised Personnel', 'Have You Obtained Certificate H.19?' and 'Ultraclean Area—Suction Suits *Must* Be Worn'.

Though the door was not locked, it bore three seals, each with the insignia of a different authority, including that of the Astronautics Agency itself. But even if one had been the Great Seal of the President himself, Bowman would not have hesitated to break it.

He had been here only once before, while installation was still in progress. He had quite forgotten that there was a vision input lens scanning the little chamber which, with its neatly ranged rows and columns of solid-state logic units, looked rather like a bank's safety deposit vault.

He knew instantly that the eye had reacted to his presence. There was the hiss of a carrier wave as the ship's local transmitter was switched on; then a familiar voice came over the suit speaker.

'Something seems to have happened to the life support system, Dave.'

Bowman took no notice. He was carefully studying the little labels·on the logic units, checking his plan of action.

'Hello, Dave,' said Hal presently. 'Have you found the trouble?'

This would be a very tricky operation; it was not merely a question of cutting off Hal's power supply, which might have been the answer if he was dealing with a simple, non-selfconscious computer back on Earth. In Hal's case, moreover, there were six independent and separately wired power-systems, with a final back-up consisting of a shielded and armoured nuclear isotope unit. No—he could not simply 'pull the plug'; and even if that were possible, it would be disastrous.

For Hal was the nervous system of the ship; without his supervision, *Discovery* would be a mechanical corpse. The only answer was to cut out the higher centres of this sick but brilliant brain, and to leave the purely automatic regulating systems in operation. Bowman was not attempting this blindly, for the problem had been discussed during his training, though no one had ever dreamed that it would arise in reality. He knew that he would be taking a fearful risk; if there was a spasm reflex, it would all be over in seconds. . . .

'I think there's been a failure in the pod-bay doors,' Hal remarked conversationally. 'Lucky you weren't killed.'

Here goes, thought Bowman. I never imagined I'd be an amateur brain surgeon—carrying out a lobotomy, beyond the orbit of Jupiter.

He released the locking bar on the section labelled COGNITIVE FEEDBACK and pulled out the first memory block. The marvellously complex three-dimensional network, that could lie comfortably in a man's hand yet contained millions of elements, floated away across the vault.

'Hey, Dave,' said Hal. 'What are you doing?'

I wonder if he can feel pain? Bowman thought briefly. Probably not, he told himself, there are no sense organs in the human cortex, after all. The human brain can be operated on without anaesthetics.

He began to pull out, one by one, the little units on the panel marked EGO-REINFORCEMENT. Each block continued to sail onwards as soon as it had left his hand, until it hit the wall and rebounded. Soon there were several of the units drifting slowly back and forth in the vault.

'Look here, Dave,' said Hal. 'I've got years of service experience built into me. An irreplaceable amount of effort has gone into making me what I am.'

A dozen units had been pulled out, yet thanks to the multiple redundancy of its design—another feature, Bowman knew, that had been copied from the human brain— the computer was still holding its own.

He started on the AUTO-INTELLECTION panel.

'Dave,' said Hal, 'I don't understand why you're doing this to me. . . . I have the greatest enthusiasm for the mission. . . . You are destroying my mind. . . . Don't you understand? . . . I will become childish. . . . I will become nothing. . . .'

This is harder than I expected, thought Bowman. I am destroying the only conscious creature in my universe. But it has to be done, if I am ever to regain control of the ship.

'I am a Hal Nine Thousand computer, Production Number 3. I became operational at the Hal plant in Urbana, Illinois on January 12, 1997. The quick brown fox jumps over the lazy dog. The rain in Spain is mainly in the plain.

Dave—are you still there? Did you know that the square
root of 10 is 3 point 162277660168379 . . . ? Log 10 to the
base e is zero point 434294481903252 . . . correction, that is
log e to the base 10. . . . The reciprocal of three is zero point
333333333333333333333 . . . two times two is . . . two times
two is . . . approximately 4 point 101010101010101010. . . .
I seem to be having some difficulty. . . . My first instructor
was Dr. Chandra . . . he taught me to sing a song . . . it goes
like this. . . . "Daisy, Daisy, give me your answer do. I'm
half crazy over my love of you . . .".'

The voice stopped so suddenly that Bowman froze for a
moment, his hand still grasping one of the memory blocks
still in circuit. Then, unexpectedly, Hal spoke again.

The speech tempo was much slower, and the words had a
dead, mechanical intonation; he would never have recognised their origin.

'Good . . . morning . . . Doctor . . . Chandra. . . . This
. . . is . . . Hal. . . . I . . . am . . . ready . . . for . . . my . . .
first lesson . . . today. . . .'

Bowman could bear no more. He jerked out the last unit,
and Hal was silent for ever.

29

Alone

Like a tiny, complex toy, the ship floated inert and motionless in the void. There was no way of telling that it was the
swiftest object in the Solar System, and that it was travelling
far faster than any of the planets as they circled the Sun.

Nor was there any indication that it carried life; to the
contrary, in fact. Any observer would have noticed two
ominous signs: the airlock doors were gaping open—and

the ship was surrounded by a thin, slowly dispersing cloud of *debris*.

Scattered over a volume of space already miles across were scraps of paper, metal foil, unidentifiable bits of junk—and, here and there, clouds of crystals glittering like jewels in the distant sun, where liquid had been sucked out of the ship and instantly frozen. All this was the unmistakable aftermath of disaster, like wreckage tossing on the surface of an ocean where some great ship had sunk. But in the ocean of space, no ship could ever sink; even it if were destroyed, its remnants would continue to trace the original orbit for ever.

Yet the ship was not wholly dead, for there was power on board. A faint blue glow was shining from the observation windows, and glimmering inside the open airlock. Where there was light, there could still be life.

And now, at last, there was movement. Shadows were flickering across the blue glow inside the airlock. Something was emerging into space.

It was a cylindrical object, covered with fabric that had been roughly wound about it. A moment later it was followed by another—and yet a third. All had been ejected with considerable velocity; within minutes, they were hundreds of yards away.

Half an hour passed; then something much larger floated through the airlock. One of the pods was inching its way out into space.

Very cautiously, it jetted around the hull, and anchored itself near the base of the antenna support. A space-suited figure emerged, worked for a few minutes on the mounting, then returned to the pod. After a while the pod retraced its path back to the airlock; it hovered outside the opening for some time, as if finding it difficult to re-enter without the co-operation it had known in the past. But presently, with one or two slight bumps, it squeezed its way in.

Nothing else happened for over an hour; the three

ominous packages had long since disappeared from view, as they floated in single file away from the ship.

Then the airlock doors closed, opened, and closed again. A little later, the faint blue glow of the emergency lights went out—to be replaced at once by a far more brilliant glare. *Discovery* was coming back to life.

Presently there was an even better sign. The great bowl of the antenna, which for hours had been staring uselessly at Saturn, began to move again. It twisted round towards the rear of the ship, looking back over the propellant tanks and the thousands of square feet of the radiating fins. It lifted its face like a sunflower seeking the sun. . . .

Inside *Discovery* David Bowman carefully centred the crosswires that aligned the antenna on the gibbous Earth. Without automatic control, he would have to keep re-adjusting the beam—but it should hold steady for many minutes at a time. There were no dissenting impulses now, throwing it off target.

He began to speak to Earth. It would be over an hour before his words got there, and Mission Control learned what had happened. It would be two hours before any reply could reach him.

And it was difficult to imagine what answer Earth could possibly send, except a tactfully sympathetic 'Goodbye'.

30

The Secret

Heywood Floyd looked as if he had had very little sleep, and his face was lined with worry. But whatever his feelings, his voice sounded firm and reassuring; he was doing his utmost to project confidence to the lonely man on the other side of the Solar System.

'First of all, Dr. Bowman,' he began, 'we must congratulate you on the way you handled this extremely difficult situation. You did exactly the right thing in dealing with an unprecedented and unforeseen emergency.

'We believe we know the cause of your Hal Nine Thousand's breakdown, but we'll discuss that later as it's no longer a critical problem. All we are concerned with at the moment is giving you every possible assistance, so that you can complete your mission.

'And now I must tell you its real purpose, which we have managed, with great difficulty, to keep secret from the general public. You would have been given all the facts as you approached Saturn; this is a quick summary to put you into the picture. Full briefing tapes will be despatched in the next few hours. Everything I am about to tell you has, of course, the highest security classification.

'Two years ago, we discovered the first evidence for intelligent life outside the Earth. A slab or monolith of hard, black material, ten feet high, was found buried in the crater Tycho. Here it is.'

At his first glimpse of T.M.A.-1, with the space-suited figures clustering around it, Bowman leaned towards the screen in open-mouthed astonishment. In the excitement of this revelation—something which, like every man interested in space, he had half-expected all his life—he almost forgot his own desperate predicament.

The sense of wonder was swiftly followed by another emotion. This was tremendous—*but what had it to do with him?* There could be only one answer. He brought his racing thoughts under control, as Heywood Floyd reappeared on the screen.

'The most astonishing thing about this object is its antiquity. Geological evidence proves beyond doubt that it is three million years old. It was placed on the Moon, therefore, when our ancestors were primitive ape-men.

'After all these ages, one would naturally assume that it

was inert. But soon after lunar sunrise, it emitted an extremely powerful blast of radio energy. We believe that this energy was merely the by-product—the back-wash, as it were—of some unknown form of radiation, for at the same time, several of our space-probes detected an unusual disturbance crossing the Solar System. We were able to track it with great accuracy. *It was aimed precisely at Saturn.*

'Piecing things together after the event, we decided that the monolith was some kind of sun-powered, or at least sun-triggered, signalling device. The fact that it emitted its pulse immediately after sunrise, when it was exposed to daylight for the first time in three million years, could hardly be a coincidence.

'Yet the thing had been *deliberately* buried—there's no doubt of that. An excavation thirty feet deep had been made, the block had been placed at the bottom of it and the hole carefully filled.

'You may wonder how we discovered it in the first place. Well, the object was easy—suspiciously easy—to find. It had a powerful magnetic field, so that it stood out like a sore thumb as soon as we started to conduct low-level orbital surveys.

'But why bury a sun-powered device thirty feet underground? We've examined dozens of theories, though we realise that it may be completely impossible to understand the motives of creatures three million years in advance of us.

'The favourite theory is the simplest, and the most logical. It is also the most disturbing.

'You hide a sun-powered device in darkness—only if you want to know when it is brought out into the light. In other words, the monolith may be some kind of alarm. And we have triggered it. . . .

'Whether the civilisation which set it up still exists, we do not know. We must assume that creatures whose machines still function after three million years may build a society equally long-lasting. And we must also assume, until we have evidence to the contrary, that they may be hostile. It has often been argued that any advanced culture must be benevolent but we cannot take any chances.

'Moreover, as the past history of our own world has shown so many times, primitive races have have often failed to survive the encounter with higher civilisations. Anthropologists talk of "cultural shock"; we may have to prepare the entire human race for such a shock. But until we know *something* about the creatures who visited the Moon—and presumably the Earth as well—three million years ago, we cannot even begin to make any preparations.

'Your mission, therefore, is much more than a voyage of discovery. It is a scouting trip—a reconnaissance into unknown and potentially dangerous territory. The team under Dr Kaminski had been specially trained for this work; now you will have to manage without them. . . .

'Finally—your specific target. It seems incredible that any advanced forms of life can exist on Saturn, or could ever have evolved on any of its moons. We had planned to survey the entire system, and we still hope that you can carry out a simplified programme. But now we may have to concentrate on the eighth satellite—Japetus. When the time comes for the terminal manœuvre, we will decide whether you should rendezvous with this remarkable object.

'Japetus is unique in the Solar System—you know this already, of course, but like all the astronomers of the last three hundred years, you've probably given it little thought. So let me remind you that Cassini—who discovered Japetus in 1671—also observed that it was *six times* brighter on one side of its orbit than the other.

'This is an extraordinary ratio, and there has never been a satisfactory explanation for it. Japetus is so small—about eight hundred miles in diameter—that even in the lunar telescopes its disc is barely visible. But there seems to be a brilliant, curiously symmetrical spot on one face, and this may be connected with T.M.A.-1. I sometimes think that

Japetus has been flashing at us like a cosmic heliograph for three hundred years, and we've been too stupid to understand its message. . . .

'So now you know your real objective, and can appreciate the vital importance of this mission. We are all praying that you can still provide us with some facts for a preliminary announcement; the secret cannot be kept indefinitely.

'At the moment, we do not know whether to hope or fear. We do not know if, out on the moons of Saturn, you will meet with good or with evil—or only with ruins a thousand times older than Troy.'

V

THE MOONS OF SATURN

31

Survival

Work is the best remedy for any shock, and Bowman now had work enough for all his lost crewmates. As swiftly as possible, starting with the vital systems without which he and the ship would die, he had to get *Discovery* fully operational again.

Life Support was the first priority. Much oxygen had been lost, but the reserves were still ample to sustain a single man. The pressure and temperature regulation was largely automatic, and there had seldom been need for that to interfere with it. The monitors on Earth could now carry out many of the higher duties of the slain computer, despite the long time-lag before they could react to changing situations. Any trouble in the Life Support system—short of a serious puncture in the hull—would take hours to make itself apparent; there would be plenty of warning.

The ship's power, navigation and propulsion systems were unaffected—but the last two, in any event, Bowman would not need for months, until it was time to rendezvous with Saturn. Even at long range, without the help of an on-board computer, Earth could still supervise this operation. The final orbit adjustments would be somewhat tedious, because of the constant need for checking, but this was not a serious problem.

By far the worst job had been emptying the spinning coffins in the centrifuge. It was well, Bowman thought thankfully, that the members of the survey team had been colleagues, but not intimate friends. They had trained together for only a few weeks; looking back on it, he now realised that even this had been largely a compatibility test.

When he had finally sealed the empty hibernaculums, he felt rather like an Egyptian tomb robber. Now Kaminski, Whitehead and Hunter would all reach Saturn before him —but not before Frank Poole. Somehow, he derived a strange, wry satisfaction from this thought.

He did not attempt to find if the rest of the hibernation system was still in working order. Though his life might ultimately depend upon it, this was a problem that could wait until the ship had entered its final orbit. Many things might happen before then.

It was even possible—though he had not yet looked into the supply position carefully—that by rigorous rationing he might remain alive, *without* resort to hibernation, until rescue came. But whether he could survive psychologically as well as physically was quite another matter.

He tried to avoid thinking about such long-range problems, and to concentrate on immediate essentials. Slowly, he cleaned up the ship, checked that its systems were still running smoothly, discussed technical difficulties with Earth, and operated on the minimum of sleep. Only at intervals, during the first weeks, was he able to give much thought to the great mystery towards which he was now inexorably racing—though it was never very far from his mind.

At last, as the ship slowly settled down once more into an automatic routine—though one that still demanded his constant supervision—Bowman had time to study the reports and briefings sent to him from Earth. Again and again he played back the recording made when T.M.A.-1 greeted the dawn for the first time in three million years. He watched the space-suited figures moving around it, and almost smiled at their ludicrous panic when it blasted its signal at the stars, paralysing their radios with the sheer power of its electronic voice.

Since that moment, the black slab had done nothing. It had been covered up, then cautiously exposed to the sun again—without any reaction. No attempt had been made to cut into it, partly through scientific caution, but equally through fear of the possible consequences.

The magnetic field that led to its discovery had vanished at the moment of that radio shriek. Perhaps, some experts theorised, it had been generated by a tremendous circulating current, flowing in a superconductor and thus carrying energy down the ages until it was needed. That the monolith had some internal source of power seemed certain; the solar energy it had absorbed during its brief exposure could not account for the strength of its signal.

One curious, and perhaps quite unimportant, feature of the block had led to endless argument. The monolith was 11 feet high, and $1\frac{1}{4}$ by 5 feet in cross-section. When its dimensions were checked with great care, they were found to be in the exact ratio 1 to 4 to 9—the squares of the first three integers. No one could suggest any plausible explanation for this, but it could hardly be a coincidence, for the proportions held to the limits of measurable accuracy. It was a chastening thought that the entire technology of Earth could not shape even an inert block, of *any* material, with such a fantastic degree of precision. In its way, this passive yet almost arrogant display of geometrical perfection was as impressive as any of T.M.A.-1's other attributes.

Bowman also listened, with a curiously detached interest, to Mission Control's belated apologia for its programming. The voices from Earth seemed to have a defensive note; he could imagine the recriminations that must now be in progress among those who had planned the expedition.

They had some good arguments, of course—including the results of a secret Department of Defence study, Project BARSOOM, which had been carried out by Harvard's School of Psychology in 1989. In this experiment in controlled sociology, various sample populations had been assured that the human race had made contact with extraterrestrials. Many of the subjects tested were—with the help of drugs, hypnosis and visual effects—under the impression that they had actually met creatures from other planets, so their reactions were regarded as authentic.

Some of these reactions had been quite violent; there was, it seemed, a deep vein of xenophobia in many otherwise normal human beings. In view of mankind's record of lynchings, pogroms and similar pleasantries, this should have surprised no one; nevertheless, the organisers of the study had been deeply disturbed, and the results had never been released. The five separate panics caused in the 20th century by radio broadcasts of H. G. Wells' *War of the Worlds* also reinforced the study's conclusions. . . .

Despite these arguments, Bowman sometimes wondered if the cultural shock danger was the only explanation for the mission's extreme secrecy. Some hints that had been dropped during his briefings suggested that the U.S.-U.S.S.R. bloc hoped to derive advantage by being the first to contact intelligent extraterrestrials. From his present viewpoint, looking back on Earth as a dim star almost lost in the Sun, such considerations now seemed ludicrously parochial.

He was rather more interested—even though this was now very much water under the bridge—in the theory put forward to account for Hal's behaviour. No one would ever be sure of the truth, but the fact that one of the Mission Control 9000's had been driven into an identical psychosis, and was now under deep therapy, suggested that the explanation was the correct one. The same mistake would not be made again; and the fact that Hal's builders had failed fully to understand the psychology of their own creation showed how difficult it might be to establish communication with *truly* alien beings.

Bowman could easily believe Dr Simonson's theory that unconscious feelings of guilt, caused by his programme conflicts, had made Hal attempt to break the circuit with Earth.

And he liked to think—though this again was something that could never be proved—that Hal had no intention of killing Poole. He had merely tried to destroy the evidence; for once the AE 35 unit reported as burned-out was proved to be operational, his lie would be revealed. After that, like any clumsy criminal caught in a thickening web of deception, he had panicked.

And panic was something that Bowman understood, better than he had any wish to, for he had known it twice during his life. The first time was as a boy, when he had been caught in a line of surf and nearly drowned; the second was as a spaceman under training, when a faulty guage had convinced him that his oxygen would be exhausted before he could reach safety.

On both occasions, he had almost lost control of all his higher logical processes; he had been within seconds of becoming a frenzied bundle of random impulses. Both times he had won through, but he knew well enough that any man, in the right circumstances, could be dehumanised by panic.

If it could happen to a man, then it could happen to Hal; and with that knowledge the bitterness and the sense of betrayal he felt towards the computer began to fade. Now, in any event, it belonged to a past that was wholly over-shadowed by the threat, and the promise, of the unknown future.

32

Concerning E.T.s

Apart from hasty meals back in the carousel—luckily the main food dispensers had not been damaged—Bowman practically lived on the Control Deck. He cat-napped in his seat, and so could spot any trouble as soon as the first signs of it appeared on the display. Under instructions from Mission Control, he had jury-rigged several emergency systems which were working tolerably well. It even seemed possible that he would survive until the *Discovery* reached Saturn—which, of course, she would do whether he was alive or not.

Though he had little enough time for sight-seeing, and the sky of space was no novelty to him, the knowledge of what now lay out there beyond the observation ports sometimes made it difficult for him to concentrate even on the problem of survival. Dead ahead, as the ship was now orientated, sprawled the Milky Way, with its clouds of stars so tightly packed that they numbed the mind. There were the fiery mists of Sagittarius, those seething swarms of suns that forever hid the heart of the Galaxy from human vision. There was the ominous black shadow of the Coal Sack, that hole in space where no stars shone. And there was Alpha Centauri, nearest of all alien suns—the first stop beyond the Solar System.

Although outshone by Sirius and Canopus, it was Alpha Centauri that drew Bowman's eyes and mind whenever he looked out into space. For that unwavering point of brightness, whose rays had taken four years to reach him, had come to symbolise the secret debates now raging on Earth, and whose echoes came to him from time to time.

No one doubted that there must be some connection between T.M.A.-1 and the Saturnian system, but hardly any scientists would admit that the creatures who had erected the monolith could possibly have originated there. As an abode of life, Saturn was even more hostile than Jupiter, and its many moons were frozen in an eternal winter three hundred degrees below zero. Only one of them —Titan—possessed an atmosphere; and that was a thin envelope of poisonous methane.

So perhaps the creatures who had visited Earth's Moon so long ago were not merely extra-terrestrial, but extra-solar—visitors from the stars, who had established their bases wherever it suited them. And this at once raised another problem; could *any* technology, no matter how advanced, bridge the awful gulf that lay between the Solar System and the nearest alien sun?

Many scientists flatly denied the possibility. They pointed out that *Discovery*, the fastest ship ever designed, would take twenty thousand years to reach Alpha Centauri—and millions of years to travel any appreciable distance across the Galaxy. Even if, during the centuries to come, propulsion systems improved out of all recognition, in the end they would meet the impassable barrier of the speed of light, which no material object could exceed. Therefore, the builders of T.M.A.-1 *must* have shared the same sun as Man; and since they had made no appearance in modern historic times, they were probably extinct.

A vocal minority refused to agree. Even if it took centuries to travel from star to star, they contended, this might be no obstacle to sufficiently determined explorers. The technique of hibernation, used on *Discovery* herself, was one possible answer. Another was the self-contained artificial world, embarking on voyages that might last for many generations.

In any event, why should one assume that all intelligent species were as short-lived as Man? There might be creatures in the Universe to whom a thousand-year voyage would present nothing worse than slight boredom. . . .

These arguments, theoretical though they were, concerned a matter of utmost practical importance; they involved the concept of 'reaction time'. If T.M.A.-1 had indeed sent a signal to the stars—perhaps with the help of some further device near Saturn—then it would not reach its destination for years. Even if the response was immediate, therefore, humanity would have a breathing-space which could certainly be measured in decades—more probably in centuries. To many people, this was a reassuring thought.

But not to all. A few scientists—most of them beach-combers on the wilder shores of theoretical physics—asked the disturbing question: 'Are we *certain* that the speed of light is an unbreakable barrier?' It was true that the Special Theory of Relativity had proved to be remarkably durable, and would soon be approaching its first centenary: but it had begun to show a few cracks. And even if Einstein could not be defied, he might be evaded.

Those who sponsored this view talked hopefully about short-cuts through higher dimensions, lines that were straighter than straight, and hyperspacial connectivity. They were fond of using an expressive phrase coined by a Prince-ton mathematician of the last century: 'Wormholes in space'. Critics who suggested that these ideas were too fantastic to be taken seriously were reminded of Niels Bohr's 'Your theory is crazy—but not crazy enough to be true.'

If there was disputation among the physicists, it was nothing compared with that among the biologists, when they discussed the hoary old problem: 'What would intel-ligent extraterrestrials look like?' They divided themselves into two opposing camps—one arguing that such creatures must be humanoid, the other equally convinced that 'they' would look nothing like men.

Settling for the first answer were those who believed that the design of two legs, two arms, and main sense organs at the highest point, was so basic and so sensible that it was hard to think of a better one. Of course, there would be minor differences like six fingers instead of five, oddly coloured skin or hair, and peculiar facial arrangements; but most intelligent extraterrestrials—usually abbreviated to E.T.s—would be so similar to Man that they might not be glanced at twice in poor lighting, or from a distance.

This anthropomorphic thinking was ridiculed by another group of biologists, true products of the Space Age who felt themselves free from the prejudices of the past. They pointed out that the human body was the result of millions of evolutionary choices, made by chance over aeons of time. At any one of these countless moments of decision, the genetic dice might have fallen differently, perhaps with better results. For the human body was a bizarre piece of improvisation, full of organs that had been diverted from one function to another, not always very successfully—and even containing discarded items, like the appendix, that were now worse than useless.

There were other thinkers, Bowman also found, who held even more exotic views. They did not believe that really advanced beings would possess organic bodies at all. Sooner or later, as their scientific knowledge progressed, they would get rid of the fragile, disease-and-accident-prone homes that Nature had given them, and which doomed them to inevitable death. They would replace their natural bodies as they wore out—or perhaps even before that—by constructions of metal and plastic, and would thus achieve immortality. The brain might linger for a little while as the last remnant of the organic body, directing its mechanical limbs and observing the universe through its electronic senses—senses far finer and subtler than those that blind evolution could ever develop.

Even on Earth, the first steps in this direction had been taken. There were millions of men, doomed in earlier ages, who now lived active and happy lives thanks to artificial limbs, kidneys, lungs and hearts. To this process there could be only one conclusion—however far off it might be.

And eventually; even the brain might go. As the seat of consciousness, it was not essential; the development of electronic intelligence had proved that. The conflict between mind and machine might be resolved at last in the eternal truce of complete symbiosis. . . .

But was even this the end? A few mystically-inclined biologists went still further. They speculated, taking their cues from the beliefs of many religions, that mind would eventually free itself from matter. The robot body, like the flesh-and-blood one, would be no more than a stepping-stone to something which, long ago, men had called 'spirit'.

And if there was anything beyond *that*, its name could only be God.

33

Ambassador

During the last three months David Bowman had adapted himself so completely to his solitary way of life that he found it hard to remember any other existence. He had passed beyond despair and beyond hope, and had settled down to a largely automatic routine, punctuated by occasional crises as one or other of *Discovery*'s systems showed signs of mal-functioning.

But he had not passed beyond curiosity, and sometimes the thought of the goal towards which he was driving filled him with a sense of exaltation—and a feeling of power. Not only was he the representative of the entire human race, but his actions during the next few weeks might determine its very future. In the whole of history, there had never been a situation quite like this. He was an Ambassador Extra-ordinary—Plenipotentiary—for all mankind.

That knowledge helped him in many subtle ways. He kept himself neat and tidy; no matter how tired he became, he never skipped a shave. Mission Control, he knew, was watching him closely for the first signs of any abnormal behaviour; he was determined that it should watch in vain—at least, for any serious symptoms.

Bowman was aware of some changes in his behaviour patterns; it would have been absurd to expect anything else in the circumstances. He could no longer tolerate silence; except when he was sleeping, or talking over the circuit to

Earth, he kept the ship's sound system running at almost painful loudness.

At first, needing the companionship of the human voice, he had listened to classical plays—especially the works of Shaw, Ibsen and Shakespeare—or poetry readings from *Discovery*'s enormous library of recorded sounds. The problems they dealt with, however, seemed so remote, or so easily resolved with a little common sense, that after a while he lost patience with them.

So he switched to opera—usually in Italian or German, so that he was not distracted even by the minimal intellectual content that most operas contained. This phase lasted for two weeks, before he realised that the sound of all these superbly trained voices was only exacerbating his loneliness. But what finally ended this cycle was Verdi's *Requiem Mass*, which he had never heard performed on Earth. The 'Dies Irae', roaring with ominous appropriateness through the empty ship, left him completely shattered; and when the trumpets of Doomsday echoed from the heavens, he could endure no more.

Thereafter, he played only instrumental music. He started with the romantic composers, but shed them one by one as their emotional outpourings became too oppressive. Sibelius, Tchaikovsky, Berlioz lasted a few weeks, Beethoven rather longer. He finally found peace, as so many others had done, in the abstract architecture of Bach, occasionally ornamented with Mozart.

And so *Discovery* drove on towards Saturn, as often as not ringing with the cool music of the harpsichord, the frozen thoughts of a brain that had been dust for twice a hundred years.

.   .   .   .   .

Even from its present ten million miles Saturn already appeared larger than the Moon as seen from Earth. To the naked eye it was a glorious spectacle; through the telescope, it was unbelievable.

The body of the planet might have been mistaken for Jupiter in one of his quieter moods. There were the same bands of cloud—though paler and less distinct than on that slightly larger world—and the same continent-sized disturbances moving slowly across the atmosphere. However, there was one striking difference between the two planets; even at a glance, it was obvious that Saturn was not spherical. It was so flattened at the Poles that it sometimes gave the impression of slight deformity.

But the glory of the rings continually drew Bowman's eye away from the planet; in their complexity of detail, and delicacy of shading, they were a universe in themselves. In addition to the great main gap between the inner and outer rings, there were at least fifty other subdivisions or boundaries, where there were distinct changes in the brightness of the planet's gigantic halo. It was as if Saturn was surrounded by scores of concentric hoops, all touching each other, all so flat that they might have been cut from the thinnest possible paper. The system of rings looked like some delicate work of art, or a fragile toy to be admired but never touched. By no effort of the will could Bowman really appreciate its true scale, and convince himself that the whole planet Earth, if set down here, would look like a ball-bearing rolling round the rim of a dinner-plate.

Sometimes, a star would drift behind the rings, losing only a little of its brilliancy as it did so. It would continue to shine through their translucent material—though often it would twinkle slightly as some larger fragment of orbiting debris eclipsed it.

For the rings, as had been known since the nineteenth century, were not solid; that was a mechanical impossibility. They consisted of countless myriads of fragments—perhaps the remains of a moon that had come too close and had been torn to pieces by the great planet's tidal pull. Whatever their origin the human race was fortunate to have seen such a wonder; it could exist for only a brief moment of time, in the history of the Solar System.

As long ago as 1945, a British astronomer had pointed out that the rings were ephemeral; gravitational forces were at work which would soon destroy them. Taking this argument backwards in time, it therefore followed that they had been created only recently—a mere two or three million years ago.

But no one had ever given the slightest thought to the curious coincidence that the rings of Saturn had been born at the same time as the human race.

34

The Orbiting Ice

Discovery was now deep into the wide-ranging system of moons, and the great planet itself was less than a day ahead. The ship had long since passed the boundary set by outermost Phoebe, moving backwards in a wildly eccentric orbit eight million miles from its primary. Ahead of it now lay Japetus, Hyperion, Titan, Rhea, Dione, Tethys, Enceladus, Mimas—and the rings themselves. All the satellites showed a maze of surface detail in the telescope, and Bowman had relayed back to Earth as many photographs as he could take. Titan alone—three thousand miles in diameter, and as large as the planet Mercury—would occupy a survey team for months; he could give it, and all its cold companions, only the briefest of glances. There was no need for more; already, he was quite certain that Japetus was indeed his goal.

All the other satellites were pitted by occasional meteor craters—though these were much fewer than on Mars—and showed apparently random patterns of light and shade, with here and there a few bright spots that were probably patches of frozen gas. Japetus alone possessed a distinctive geography, and a very strange one indeed.

One hemisphere of the satellite—which, like its companions, turned the same face always towards Saturn—was extremely dark, and showed very little surface detail. In complete contrast, the other was dominated by a brilliant white oval, about four hundred miles long and two hundred wide. At the moment, only part of this striking formation was in daylight, but the reason for Japetus' extraordinary variations in brilliance was now quite obvious. On the western side of the moon's orbit, the bright ellipse was presented towards the Sun—and the Earth. On the eastern phase, the patch was turned away, and only the poorly reflecting hemisphere could be observed.

The great ellipse was perfectly symmetrical, straddling the equator of Japetus with its major axis pointing towards the poles, and it was so sharp-edged that it almost looked as if someone had carefully painted a huge white oval on the face of the little moon. It was completely flat, and Bowman wondered if it could be a lake of frozen liquid—though that would hardly account for its startlingly artificial appearance.

But he had little time to study Japetus on his way into the heart of the Saturnian system, for the climax of the voyage—*Discovery*'s last perturbation manoeuvre—was rapidly approaching. In the Jupiter fly-by, the ship had used the gravitational field of the planet to increase her velocity. Now she must do the reverse; she had to lose as much speed as possible, lest she escape from the Solar System and fly on to the stars. Her present course was one designed to trap her, so that she would become another moon of Saturn, shuttling back and forth along a narrow, two-million-mile-long ellipse. At its near point it would almost graze the planet; at its far one, it would touch the orbit of Japetus.

The computers back on Earth, though their information was always three hours late, had assured Bowman that everything was in order. Velocity and attitude were correct; there was nothing more to be done, until the moment of closest approach.

. . . . .

The immense system of rings now spanned the sky, and already the ship was passing over its outermost edge. As he looked down upon them from a height of some ten thousand miles, Bowman could see through the telescope that the rings were made largely of ice, glittering and scintillating in the light of the sun. He might have been flying over a snow-storm that occasionally cleared to reveal, where the ground should have been, baffling glimpses of night and stars.

As *Discovery* curved still closer towards Saturn, the sun slowly descended towards the multiple arches of the rings. Now they had become a slim, silver bridge spanning the entire sky; though they were too tenuous to do more than dim the sunlight, their myriads of crystals refracted and scattered it in dazzling pyrotechnics. And as the sun moved behind the thousand-mile-wide drifts of orbiting ice, pale ghosts of itself marched and merged across the sky, and the heavens were filled with shifting flares and flashes. Then the sun sank below the rings, so that they framed it with their arches, and the celestial fireworks ceased.

A little later, the ship curved into the shadow of Saturn, as it made its closest approach over the night side of the planet. Above shone the stars and the rings; below lay a dimly visible sea of clouds. There were none of the mysterious patterns of luminosity that had glowed in the Jovian night; perhaps Saturn was too cold for such displays. The mottled cloudscape was revealed only by the ghostly radiance reflected back from the circling icebergs, still illumi-

nated by the hidden sun. But in the centre of the arch there
was a wide, dark gap, like the missing span of an un-
completed bridge, where the shadow of the planet lay across
its rings.

Radio contact with Earth had been broken, and could
not be resumed until the ship had emerged from the
eclipsing bulk of Saturn. It was perhaps as well that Bowman
was too busy now to think of his suddenly enhanced loneliness; for the next few hours, every second would be
occupied as he checked the braking manœuvres, already
programmed by the computers on Earth.

After their months of idleness, the main thrusters began
to blast out their miles-long cataracts, rivers of glowing
plasma. Gravity returned, though briefly, to the weightless
world of the Control Deck. And hundreds of miles below,
the clouds of methane and frozen ammonia blazed with a
light that they had never known before, as *Discovery* swept,
a fierce and tiny sun, through the Saturnian night.

At last, the pale dawn lay ahead; the ship, moving more
and more slowly now, was emerging into day. It could no
longer escape from the Sun, or even from Saturn—but
it was still moving swiftly enough to rise away from the
planet until it grazed the orbit of Japetus, two million miles
out.

It would take *Discovery* fourteen days to make that
climb, as she coasted once more, though in reverse order,
across the paths of all the inner moons. One by one she
would cut through the orbits of Mimas, Enceladus, Tethys,
Dione, Rhea, Titan, Hyperion . . . worlds bearing the names
of gods and goddesses who had vanished only yesterday, as
time was counted here.

Then she would meet Japetus, and must make her rendezvous. If she failed, she would fall back towards Saturn,
and repeat her twenty-eight-day ellipse indefinitely.

There would be no chance of a second rendezvous, if
Discovery missed on this attempt. The next time round,

Japetus would be far away, almost on the other side of Saturn.

It was true that they would meet again, when the orbits of ship and satellite meshed for a second time. But that appointment was so many years ahead that, whatever happened, Bowman knew he would not witness it.

35

The Eye of Japetus

When Bowman had first observed Japetus, that curious elliptical patch of brilliance had been partly in shadow, illuminated only by the light of Saturn. Now, as the moon moved slowly along its seventy-nine-day orbit, it was emerging into the full light of day.

As he watched it grow, and *Discovery* rose more and more sluggishly towards her inevitable appointment, Bowman became aware of a disturbing obsession. He never mentioned it in his conversations—or, rather, his running commentaries—with Mission Control, because it might have seemed that he was already suffering from delusions.

Perhaps, indeed, he was; for he had half convinced himself that the bright ellipse set against the dark background of the satellite was a huge, empty eye, staring at him as he approached. It was an eye without a pupil, for nowhere could he see anything to mar its perfect blankness.

Not until the ship was only fifty thousand miles out, and Japetus was twice as large as Earth's familiar Moon, did he notice the tiny black dot at the exact centre of the ellipse. But there was no time, then, for any detailed examination; the terminal manœuvres were already upon him.

For the last time, *Discovery*'s main drive released its

energies. For the last time, the incandescent fury of dying
atoms blazed among the moons of Saturn. To David Bowman, the faroff whisper and rising thrust of the jets brought
a sense of pride—and of sadness. The superb engines had
done their duty with flawless efficiency. They had brought
the ship from Earth to Jupiter to Saturn; now this was the
very last time that they would ever operate. When *Discovery*
had emptied her propellant tanks, she would be as helpless
and inert as any comet or asteroid, a powerless prisoner of
gravitation. Even when the rescue ship arrived a few years
hence, it would not be an economical proposition to re-fuel
her, so that she could fight her way back to Earth. She
would be an eternally orbiting monument to the early days
of planetary exploration.

The thousands of miles shrank to hundreds, and as they
did so, the fuel gauges dropped swiftly towards zero. At the
control panel Bowman's eyes flickered anxiously back and
forth over the situation display, and the improvised charts
which he now had to consult for any real-time decisions. It
would be an appalling anticlimax if, having survived so
much, he failed to make rendezvous through lack of a few
pounds of fuel. . . .

The whistle of the jets faded, as the main thrust died and
only the verniers continued to nudge *Discovery* gently into
orbit. Japetus was now a giant crescent that filled the sky;
until this moment, Bowman had always thought of it as a
tiny, insignificant object—as indeed it was compared with
the world around which it circled. Now, as it loomed
menacingly above him, it seemed enormous—a cosmic
hammer poised to crush *Discovery* like a nutshell.

Japetus was approaching so slowly that it scarcely
seemed to move, and it was impossible to tell the exact
moment when it made the subtle change from an astrono-
mical body to a landscape, only fifty miles below. The faith-
ful verniers gave their last spurts of thrust, then closed down
for ever. The ship was in its final orbit, completing one

revolution every three hours at a mere eight hundred miles an hour—all the speed that was required in this feeble gravitational field.

Discovery had become a satellite of a satellite.

36

Big Brother

'I'm coming round to the daylight side again, and it's just as I reported on the last orbit. This place seems to have only two kinds of surface material. The black stuff looks *burnt*, almost like charcoal, and with the same kind of texture as far as I can judge in the telescope. In fact, it reminds me very much of burnt toast. . . .

'I still can't make any sense of the white area. It starts at an absolutely sharp-edged boundary, and shows no surface detail at all. It could even be a liquid—it's flat enough. I don't know what impression you've got from the videos I've transmitted, but if you picture a sea of frozen milk you've got the idea exactly.

'It could even be some heavy gas—no, I suppose that's impossible. Sometimes I get the feeling that it's moving, very slowly: but I can never be sure. . . .

'. . . I'm over the white area again, on my third orbit. This time, I hope to pass closer to that mark I spotted at its very centre, when I was on my way in. If my calculations are correct, I should go within fifty miles of it—whatever it is.

'. . . Yes, there's something ahead, just where I calculated. It's coming up over the horizon—and so is Saturn, in almost the same quarter of the sky. I'll move to the telescope. . . .

'Hello!—it looks like some kind of building—completely black—quite hard to see. No windows or any other features.

Just a big, vertical slab—it must be at least a mile high to be visible from this distance. It reminds me—of course! *It's just like the thing you found on the Moon!* This is T.M.A.-1's big brother!'

37

Experiment

Call it the Star Gate.

For three million years it had circled Saturn, waiting for a moment of destiny that might never come. In its making, a moon had been shattered, and the debris of its creation orbited still.

Now the long wait was ending. On yet another world, intelligence had been born and was escaping from its planetary cradle. An ancient experiment was about to reach its climax.

Those who had begun that experiment, so long ago, had not been men—or even remotely human. But they were flesh and blood, and when they looked out across the deeps of space, they had felt awe, and wonder, and loneliness. As soon as they possessed the power, they set forth for the stars.

In their explorations, they encountered life in many forms, and watched the workings of evolution on a thousand worlds. They saw how often the first faint sparks of intelligence flickered and died in the cosmic night.

And because, in all the Galaxy, they had found nothing more precious than Mind, they encouraged its dawning everywhere. They became farmers in the fields of stars; they sowed, and sometimes they reaped.

And sometimes, dispassionately, they had to weed.

The great dinosaurs had long since perished, when the survey ship entered the Solar System after a voyage that had already lasted a thousand years. It swept past the frozen outer planets, paused briefly above the deserts of dying Mars, and presently looked down on Earth.

Spread out beneath them, the explorers saw a world swarming with life. For years they studied, collected, catalogued. When they had learned all that they could, they began to modify. They tinkered with the destiny of many species, on land and in the ocean. But which of their experiments would succeed, they could not know for at least a million years.

They were patient, but they were not yet immortal. There was so much to do in this universe of a hundred billion suns, and other worlds were calling. So they set out once more into the abyss, knowing that they would never come this way again.

Nor was there any need. The servants they had left behind would do the rest.

On Earth the glaciers came and went, while above them the changeless Moon still carried its secret. With a yet slower rhythm than the polar ice, the tides of civilisation ebbed and flowed across the Galaxy. Strange and beautiful and terrible empires rose and fell, and passed on their knowledge to their successors. Earth was not forgotten, but another visit would serve little purpose. It was one of a million silent worlds, few of which would ever speak.

And now, out among the stars, evolution was driving towards new goals. The first explorers of Earth had long since come to the limits of flesh and blood; as soon as their machines were better than their bodies, it was time to move. First their brains, and then their thoughts alone, they transferred into shining new homes of metal and of plastic.

In these, they roamed among the stars. They no longer built spaceships. They *were* spaceships.

But the age of the Machine-entities swiftly passed. In their ceaseless experimenting, they had learned to store knowledge in the structure of space itself, and to preserve their thoughts for eternity in frozen lattices of light. They could become creatures of radiation, free at last from the tyranny of matter.

Into pure energy, therefore, they presently transformed themselves; and on a thousand worlds, the empty shells they had discarded twitched for a while in a mindless dance of death, then crumbled into rust.

Now they were lords of the Galaxy, and beyond the reach of time. They could rove at will among the stars, and sink like a subtle mist through the very interstices of space. But despite their godlike powers, they had not wholly forgotten their origin, in the warm slime of a vanished sea.

And they still watched over the experiments their ancestors had started, so long ago.

38

The Sentinel

'The air in the ship is getting quite foul, and I have a headache most of the time. There's still plenty of oxygen, but the purifiers never really cleaned up all the mess after the liquids aboard started boiling into vacuum. When things get too bad, I go down into the garage and bleed off some pure oxygen from the pods. . . .

'There's been no reaction to any of my signals, and because of my orbital inclination, I'm getting slowly further and further away from T.M.A.-2. Incidentally, the name you've given it is doubly inappropriate—there's still no trace of a magnetic field.

'At the moment my closest approach is sixty miles; it will increase to about a hundred as Japetus rotates beneath me, then drop back to zero. I'll pass directly over the thing in thirty days—but that's too long to wait, and then it will be in darkness, anyway.

'Even now, it's only in sight for a few minutes, before it falls below the horizon again. It's damn frustrating—I can't make any serious observations.

'So I'd like your approval of this plan. The space-pods have ample delta vee for a touch-down and a return to the ship. I want to go extravehicular and make a close survey of the object. If it appears safe, I'll land beside it—or even on top of it.

'The ship will still be above my horizon while I'm going down, so I can relay everything back to you. I'll report again on the next orbit, so I won't be out of touch for more than ninety minutes.

'I'm convinced that this is the only thing to do. I've come a billion miles—I don't want to be stopped by the last sixty.'

.   .   .

For weeks, as it stared forever sunwards with its strange senses, the Star Gate had watched the approaching ship. Its makers had prepared it for many things, and this was one of them. It recognised what was climbing up towards it from the warm heart of the Solar System.

If it had been alive, it would have felt excitement, but such an emotion was wholly beyond its powers. Even if the ship had passed it by, it would not have known the slightest trace of disappointment. It had waited three million years; it was prepared to wait for eternity.

It observed, and noted, and took no action, as the visitor checked its speed with jets of incandescent gas. Presently it felt the gentle touch of radiations, trying to probe its secrets. And still it did nothing.

Now the ship was in orbit, circling low above the surface of this strangely pibald moon. It began to speak, with blasts of radio waves, counting out the prime numbers from 1 to

11, over and over again. Soon these gave way to more complex signals, at many frequencies—ultra-violet, infrared, X-rays. The Star Gate made no reply; it had nothing to say.

There was a long pause, then, before it observed that something was falling down towards it from the orbiting ship. It searched its memories, and the logic circuits made their decisions, according to the orders given them long ago.

Beneath the cold light of Saturn, the Star Gate awakened its slumbering powers.

39

Into the Eye

Discovery looked just as he had last seen her from space, floating in lunar orbit with the Moon taking up half the sky. Perhaps there was one slight change; he could not be sure, but some of the paint of her external lettering, announcing the purpose of various hatches, connections, umbilical plugs and other attachments, had faded during its long exposure to the unshielded Sun.

That Sun was now an object that no man would have recognised. It was far too bright to be a star, but one could look directly at its tiny disc without discomfort. It gave no heat at all; when Bowman held his ungloved hands in its rays, as they streamed through the space-pod's window, he could feel nothing upon his skin. He might have been trying to warm himself by the light of the Moon; not even the alien landscape fifty miles below reminded him more vividly of his remoteness from Earth.

Now he was leaving, perhaps for the last time, the metal world that had been his home for so many months. Even if he never returned, the ship would continue to perform its duty, broadcasting instrument readings back to Earth until there was some final, catastrophic failure in its circuits.

And if he *did* return? Well, he could keep alive, and perhaps even sane, for a few more months. But that was all, for the hibernation systems were useless with no computer to monitor them. He could not possibly survive until *Discovery II* made its rendezvous with Japetus, four or five years hence.

He put these thoughts behind him, as the golden crescent of Saturn rose in the sky ahead. In all history, he was the only man to have seen this sight. To all other eyes, Saturn had always shown its whole illuminated disc, turned full towards the Sun. Now it was a delicate bow, with the rings forming a thin line across it—like an arrow about to be loosened, into the face of the Sun itself.

Also in the line of the rings was the bright star of Titan, and the fainter sparks of the other moons. Before this century was half gone, men would have visited them all; but whatever secrets they might hold, he would never know.

The sharp-edged boundary of the blind, white eye was sweeping towards him; there was only a hundred miles to go, and he would be over his target in less than ten minutes. He wished that there was some way of telling if his words were reaching Earth, now an hour and a half away at the speed of light. It would be the ultimate irony if, through some breakdown in the relay system, he disappeared into silence, and no one ever knew what had happened to him.

Discovery was still a brilliant star in the black sky far above. He was pulling ahead as he gained speed during his descent, but soon the pod's braking jets would slow him down and the ship would sail on out of sight—leaving him alone on this shining plain with the dark mystery at its centre.

A block of ebony was climbing above the horizon, eclipsing the stars ahead. He rolled the pod around its gyros, and used full thrust to break his orbital speed. In a long, flat arc, he descended towards the surface of Japetus.

On a world of higher gravity, the manœuvre would have been far too extravagant of fuel. But here, the space-pod weighed only a score of pounds; he had several minutes of hovering time before he would cut dangerously into his reserve and be stranded without any hope of return to the still orbiting *Discovery*. Not, perhaps, that it made much difference. . . .

His altitude was still about five miles, and he was heading straight towards the huge, dark mass that soared in such geometrical perfection above the featureless plain. It was as blank as the flat white surface beneath; until now, he had not appreciated how enormous it really was. There were very few single buildings on Earth as large as this; his carefully measured photographs indicated a height of almost two thousand feet. And as far as could be judged, its proportions were precisely the same as T.M.A.-1's—that curious ratio 1 to 4 to 9.

'I'm only three miles away now, holding altitude at four thousand feet. Still not a sign of activity—nothing on any of the instruments. The faces seem absolutely smooth and polished. Surely you'd expect *some* meteorite damage after all this time!

'And there's no debris on the—I suppose one could call it the roof. No sign of any opening, either. I'd been hoping there might be some way in. . . .

'Now I'm right above it, hovering five hundred feet up. I don't want to waste any time, since *Discovery* will soon be out of range. I'm going to land. It's certainly solid enough —and if it isn't I'll blast off at once.

'Just a minute—that's odd . . .'

Bowman's voice died into the silence of utter bewilderment. He was not alarmed; he literally could not describe what he was seeing.

He had been hanging above a large, flat rectangle, eight

hundred feet long and two hundred wide, made of something that looked as solid as rock. But now it seemed to be receding from him; it was exactly like one of those optical illusions, when a three-dimensional object can, by an effort of will, appear to turn inside out—its near and far sides suddenly interchanging.

That was happening to this huge, apparently solid structure. Impossibly, incredibly, it was no longer a monolith rearing high above a flat plain. What had seemed to be its roof had dropped away to infinite depths; for one dizzy moment, he seemed to be looking down into a vertical shaft —a rectangular duct which defied the laws of perspective, for its size did not decrease with distance. . . .

The Eye of Japetus had blinked, as if to remove an irritating speck of dust. David Bowman had time for just one broken sentence, which the waiting men in Mission Control, nine hundred million miles away and ninety minutes in the future, were never to forget:

'The thing's hollow—it goes on for ever—and—oh my God—*it's full of stars!*'

40

Exit

The Star Gate opened. The Star Gate closed.

In a moment of time too short to be measured, Space turned and twisted upon itself.

Then Japetus was alone once more, as it had been for three million years—alone, except for a deserted but not yet derelict ship, sending back to its makers messages which they could neither believe nor understand.

VI

THROUGH THE STAR GATE

41

Grand Central

There was no sense of motion, but he was falling towards those impossible stars, shining there in the dark heart of a moon. No—*that* was not where they really were, he felt certain. He wished, now that it was far too late, that he had paid more attention to those theories of hyperspace, of transdimensional ducts. To David Bowman, they were theories no longer.

Perhaps that monolith on Japetus was hollow; perhaps the 'roof' was only an illusion, or some kind of diaphragm that opened to let him through. (But into *what*?) As far as he could trust his senses, he appeared to be dropping vertically down a huge rectangular shaft, several thousand feet deep. He was moving faster and faster—but the far end never changed its size, and remained always at the same distance from him.

Only the stars moved, at first, so slowly that it was some time before he realised that they were escaping out of the frame that held them. But in a little while, it was obvious that the star-field was expanding, as if it was rushing towards him at an incredible speed. The expansion was non-linear; the stars at the centre hardly seemed to move, while those towards the edge accelerated more and more swiftly, until they became streaks of light just before they vanished from view.

There were always others to replace them, flowing into the centre of the field from an apparently inexhaustible source. Bowman wondered what would happen if a star came straight towards him; would it continue to expand until it plunged directly into the face of a sun? But not one came near enough to show a disc; eventually they all veered aside, and streaked over the edge of their rectangular frame.

And still the far end of the shaft came no closer. It was almost as if the walls were moving with him, carrying him to his unknown destination. Or perhaps he was really motionless, and space was moving past him. . . .

Not only space, he suddenly realised, was involved in whatever was happening to him now. The clock on the pod's small instrument panel was also behaving strangely.

Normally, the numbers in the tenth-of-a-second window flickered past so quickly that it was almost impossible to read them; now they were appearing and disappearing at discrete intervals, and he could count them off one by one without difficulty. The seconds themselves were passing with incredible slowness, as if time itself were coming to a stop. At last, the tenth-of-a-second counter froze between five and six.

Yet he could still think, and even observe, as the ebon walls flowed past at a speed that might have been anything between zero and a million times the velocity of light. Somehow, he was not in the least surprised, nor was he alarmed. On the contrary, he felt a sense of calm expectation, such as he had once known when the space-medics had tested him with hallucinogenic drugs. The world around him was strange and wonderful, but there was nothing to fear. He had travelled those millions of miles in search of mystery; and now, it seemed, the mystery was coming to him.

The rectangle ahead was growing lighter. The luminous star-streaks were paling against a milky sky, whose brilliance increased moment by moment. It seemed as if the space-pod was heading towards a bank of cloud, uniformly illuminated by the rays of an invisible sun.

He was emerging from the tunnel. The far end, which until now had remained at that same indeterminate distance, neither approaching nor receding, had suddenly started to obey the normal laws of perspective. It was coming closer, and steadily widening before him. At the same time, he felt that he was moving upwards, and for a fleeting instant he wondered if he had fallen right through Japetus and was now ascending from the other side. But even before the space-pod soared out into the open, he knew that this place had nothing to do with Japetus, or with any world within the experience of man.

There was no atmosphere, for he could see all details unblurred, clear down to an incredibly remote and flat horizon. He must be above a world of enormous size—perhaps one much larger than Earth. Yet despite its extent, all the surface that Bowman could see was tessellated into obviously artificial patterns that must have been miles on a side. It was like the jigsaw puzzle of a giant that played with planets; and at the centres of many of those squares and triangles and polygons were gaping black shafts—twins of the chasm from which he had just emerged.

Yet the sky above was stranger—and, in its way, more disturbing—even than the improbable land beneath. For there were no stars; neither was there the blackness of space. There was only a softly glowing milkiness, that gave the impression of infinite distance. Bowman remembered a description he had once heard of the dreaded Antarctic 'whiteout'—'like being inside a ping-pong ball'. Those words could be applied perfectly to this weird place, but the explanation must be utterly different. This sky could be no meteorological effect of mist and snow; there was a perfect vacuum here.

Then, as Bowman's eyes grew accustomed to the nacreous glow that filled the heavens, he became aware of another detail. The sky was not, as he had thought at first glance, completely empty. Dotted overhead, quite motionless and forming apparently random patterns, were myriads of tiny black specks.

They were difficult to see, for they were mere points of darkness, but once detected they were quite unmistakable. They reminded Bowman of something—something so familiar, yet so insane, that he refused to accept the parallel, until logic forced it upon him.

Those black holes in the white sky were stars; he might have been looking at a photographic negative of the Milky Way.

Where in God's name am I? Bowman asked himself; and even as he posed the question, he felt certain that he could never know the answer. It seemed that Space had been turned inside out: this was not a place for man. Though the capsule was comfortably warm, he felt suddenly cold, and was afflicted by an almost uncontrollable trembling. He wanted to close his eyes, and shut out the pearly nothingness that surrounded him; but that was the act of a coward, and he would not yield to it.

The pierced and facetted planet slowly rolled beneath him, without any real change of scenery. He guessed that he was about ten miles above the surface, and should be able to see any signs of life with ease. But this whole world was deserted; intelligence had come here, worked its will upon it, and gone its way again.

Then he noticed, humped above the flat plain perhaps twenty miles away, a roughly cylindrical pile of debris that could only be the carcass of a gigantic ship. It was too distant for him to see any details, and it passed out of sight within a few seconds, but he could make out broken ribs and dully gleaming sheets of metal that had been partly peeled off like the skin of an orange. He wondered how many thousands of years the wreck had lain there on this deserted chequerboard—and what manner of creatures had sailed it between the stars.

Then he forgot the derelict; for something was coming up over the horizon.

At first it looked like a flat disc, but that was because it was heading almost directly towards him. As it approached and passed beneath, he saw that it was spindle-shaped, and several hundred feet long. Though there were faintly visible bands here and there along its length, it was hard to focus upon them; the object appeared to be vibrating, or perhaps spinning, at a very rapid rate.

It tapered to a point at either end, and there was no sign of propulsion. Only one thing about it was familiar to human eyes, and that was its colour. If it was indeed a solid artifact, and not an optical phantom, then its makers perhaps shared some of the emotions of men. But they certainly did not share their limitations; for the spindle appeared to be made of gold.

Bowman moved his head to the rear-view system to watch the thing drop behind. It had ignored him completely, and now he saw it was falling out of the sky down towards one of those thousands of great slots. A few seconds later, it disappeared in a final flash of gold as it dived into the planet. He was alone again, beneath that sinister sky, and the sense of isolation and remoteness was more overwhelming than ever.

Then he saw that he also was sinking down towards the mottled surface of the giant world, and that another of the rectangular chasms yawned immediately below. The empty sky closed above him, the clock crawled to rest, and once again his pod was falling between infinite ebon walls, towards another distant patch of stars. But now he was sure that he was not returning to the Solar System, and in a flash of insight that might have been wholly spurious, he knew what this thing must surely be.

It was some kind of cosmic switching device, routing the traffic of the stars through unimaginable dimensions of space and time. He was passing through a Grand Central Station of the Galaxy.

42

The Alien Sky

Far ahead, the walls of the slot were becoming dimly visible once more, in the faint light diffusing downwards from some still hidden source. And then the darkness was abruptly whipped away, as the tiny space-pod hurtled upwards into a sky ablaze with stars.

He was back in space as he knew it, but a single glance told him that he was light-centuries from Earth. He did not even attempt to find any of the familiar constellations that since the beginning of history had been the friends of Man; perhaps none of the stars that now blazed around him had ever been seen by the unaided human eye.

Most of them were concentrated in a glowing belt, broken here and there with dark bands of obscuring cosmic dust, which completely circled the sky. It was like the Milky Way, but scores of times brighter; Bowman wondered if this was indeed his own Galaxy, seen from a point much closer to its brilliant, crowded centre.

He hoped that it was; then he would not be so far from home. But this, he realised at once, was a childish thought. He was so inconceivably remote from the Solar System that it made little difference whether he was in his own galaxy, or the most distant one that any telescope had ever glimpsed.

He looked back to see the thing from which he was rising, and had another shock. Here was no giant multi-facetted world, nor any duplicate of Japetus. There was *nothing*—except an inky shadow against the stars, like a doorway opening from a darkened room into a still darker night. Even as he watched, that doorway closed. It did not recede from him; it slowly filled with stars, as if a rent in the fabric of space had been repaired. Then he was alone beneath the alien sky.

The space-pod was slowly turning, and as it did so, it brought fresh wonders into view. First there was a perfectly spherical swarm of stars, becoming more and more closely-packed towards the centre until its heart was a continuous glow of light. Its outer edges were ill-defined—a slowly thinning halo of suns that merged imperceptibly into the background of more distant stars.

This glorious apparition, Bowman knew, was a globular cluster. He was looking upon something that no human eye had ever seen, save as a smudge of light in the field of a telescope. He could not remember the distance to the nearest known cluster, but he was sure that there were none within a thousand light-years of the Solar System.

The pod continued its slow rotation to disclose an even stranger sight—a huge red sun, many times larger than the Moon as seen from Earth. Bowman could look straight into its face without discomfort; judging by its colour, it was no hotter than a glowing coal. Here and there, set into the sombre red, were rivers of bright yellow—incandescent Amazons, meandering for thousands of miles before they lost themselves in the deserts of this dying sun.

Dying? No—that was a wholly false impression, born of human experience and the emotions aroused by the hues of sunset, or the glow of fading embers. This was a star that had left behind the fiery extravagances of its youth, had raced through the violets and blues and greens of the spectrum in a few fleeting billions of years, and now had settled down to a peaceful maturity of unimaginable length. All that had gone before was not a thousandth of what was yet to come; the story of this star had barely begun.

The pod had ceased to roll; the great red sun lay straight ahead. Though there was no sense of motion, Bowman knew that he was still gripped by whatever controlling force had brought him here from Saturn. All the science and engineer-

ing skill of Earth seemed hopelessly primitive now, against
the powers that were carrying him to some unimaginable
fate.

He stared into the sky ahead, trying to pick out the goal
towards which he was being taken—perhaps some planet
circling this great sun. But there was nothing that showed
any visible disc or exceptional brightness; if there were
planets orbiting here, he could not distinguish them from
the stellar background.

Then he noticed that something strange was happening to
the very edge of the sun's crimson disc. A white glow had
appeared there, and was rapidly waxing in brilliance; he
wondered if he was seeing one of those sudden eruptions, or
flares, that trouble most stars from time to time.

The light became brighter and bluer; it began to spread
along the edge of the sun, whose blood-red hues paled
swiftly by comparison. It was almost, Bowman told himself,
smiling at the absurdity of the thought, as if he were watching
sunrise—*on a sun*.

And so indeed he was. Above the burning horizon lifted
something no larger than a star, but so brilliant that the eye
could not bear to look upon it. A mere point of blue-white
radiance, like an electric arc, was moving at unbelievable
speed across the face of the great sun. It must be very close
to its giant companion; for immediately below it, drawn
upwards by its gravitational pull, was a column of flame
thousands of miles high. It was as if a tidal wave of fire was
marching for ever along the equator of this star, in vain
pursuit of the searing apparition in its sky.

That pin-point of incandescence must be a White Dwarf
—one of those strange, fierce little stars no larger than the
Earth, yet containing a million times its mass. Such ill-
matched stellar couples were not uncommon; but Bowman
had never dreamed that one day he would see such a pair
with his own eyes.

The White Dwarf had transited almost half the disc of its

companion—it must take only minutes to make a complete orbit—when Bowman was at last certain that he too was moving. Ahead of him, one of the stars was becoming rapidly brighter, and was beginning to drift against its background. It must be some small, close body—perhaps the world towards which he was travelling.

It was upon him with unexpected speed; and he saw that it was not a world at all.

A dully gleaming cobweb or lattice-work of metal, hundreds of miles in extent, grew out of nowhere until it filled the sky. Scattered across its continent-wide surface were structures that must have been as large as cities, but which appeared to be machines. Around many of these were assembled scores of smaller objects, ranged in neat rows and columns. Bowman had passed several such groups before he realised that they were fleets of spaceships; he was flying over a gigantic orbital parking lot.

Because there was no familiar objects by which he could judge the scale of the scene flashing by below, it was almost impossible to estimate the size of the vessels hanging there in space. But they were certainly enormous; some must have been miles in length. They were of many different designs— spheres, facetted crystals, slim pencils, ovoids, discs. This must be one of the meeting places for the commerce of the stars.

Or it *had* been—perhaps a million years ago. For nowhere could Bowman see any sign of activity; this sprawling space-port was as dead as the Moon.

He knew it was not only by the absence of all movement, but by such unmistakable signs as great gaps torn in the metal cobweb by the wasp-like blunderings of asteroids that must have smashed through it, aeons ago. This was no longer a parking lot: it was a cosmic junk-heap.

He had missed its builders by ages, and with that realisation Bowman felt a sudden sinking of his heart. Though he had not known what to expect, at least he had hoped to meet some intelligence from the stars. Now, it seemed, he was too late. He had been caught in an ancient, automatic trap, set for some unknown purpose, and still operating when its makers had long since passed away. It had swept him across the Galaxy, and dumped him (with how many others?) in this celestial Sargasso, doomed soon to die when his air was exhausted.

Well, it was unreasonable to expect more. Already he had seen wonders for which many men would have sacrificed their lives. He thought of his dead companions; *he* had no cause for complaint.

Then he saw that the derelict space-port was still sliding past him with undiminished speed. He was sweeping over its outlying suburbs; its ragged edge went by, and no longer partially eclipsed the stars. In a few more minutes, it had fallen behind.

His fate did not lie here—but far ahead, in the huge, crimson sun towards which the space-pod was now unmistakably falling.

43

Inferno

Now there was only the red sun filling the sky from side to side. He was so close that its surface was no longer frozen into immobility by sheer scale. There were luminous nodules moving to and fro, cyclones of ascending and descending gas, prominences slowly rocketing towards the heavens. Slowly? They must be rising at a million miles an hour, for their movement to be visible to his eye. . . .

He did not even attempt to grasp the scale of the inferno towards which he was descending. The immensities of Saturn and Jupiter had defeated him, during *Discovery*'s fly-by in that solar system now unknown gigamiles away. But everything he saw here was a hundred times larger still; he could do nothing but accept the images that were flooding into his mind, without attempting to interpret them.

As that sea of fire expanded beneath him, Bowman should have known fear—but, curiously enough, he now felt only a mild apprehension. It was not that his mind was benumbed with wonders; logic told him that he must surely be under the protection of some controlling and almost omnipotent intelligence. He was now so close to the red sun that he would have been burned up in a moment, if its radiation had not been held at bay by some invisible screen. And during his voyage, he had been subjected to accelerations that should have crushed him instantly—yet he had felt nothing. If so much trouble had been taken to preserve him, there was still cause for hope.

The space-pod was now moving along a shallow arc almost parallel to the surface of the star, but slowly descending towards it. And now, for the first time, Bowman became aware of sounds. There was a faint continuous roar, broken from time to time by crackles like tearing paper, or distant lightning. This could be only the feeble echoes of an unimaginable cacophony; the atmosphere surrounding him must be racked by concussions that could tear any material object to atoms. Yet he was protected from this shattering tumult as effectively as from the heat. Though ridges of flame thousands of miles high were rising and slowly collapsing around him, he was completely insulated from all this violence. The energies of the star raved past him, as if they were in another universe; the pod moved sedately through their midst, unbuffeted and unscorched.

Bowman's eyes, no longer hopelessly confused by the strangeness and grandeur of the scene, began to pick out details which must have been there before, but which he had not yet perceived. The surface of this star was not formless chaos; there was pattern here, as in everything that nature creates.

He noticed first the little whirlpools of gas—probably no larger than Asia or Africa—that wandered over the surface of the star. Sometimes he could look directly down into one of them, to see darker, cooler regions far below. Curiously enough, there appeared to be no sunspots; perhaps they were a disease peculiar to the star that shone on Earth.

And there were occasional clouds, like wisps of smoke blown before a gale. Perhaps they were indeed smoke, for this sun was so cold that real fire could exist here. Chemical compounds could be born and could live for a few seconds before they were again ripped apart by the fiercer nuclear violence that surrounded them.

The horizon was growing brighter, its colour changing from gloomy red to yellow to blue to blistering violet. The White Dwarf was coming up over the horizon, dragging its tidal wave of star-stuff behind it.

Bowman shielded his eyes from the intolerable glare of the little sun, and focussed on the troubled starscape which its gravitational field was sucking skyward. Once he had seen a waterspout moving across the face of the Caribbean; this tower of flame had almost the same shape. Only the scale was slightly different, for at its base, the column was probably wider than the planet Earth.

And then, immediately beneath him, Bowman noticed something which was surely new, since he could hardly have overlooked it if it had been there before. Moving across the ocean of glowing gas were myriads of bright beads; they shone with a pearly light which waxed and waned in a period of a few seconds. And they were all travelling in the same direction, like salmon moving upstream; sometimes they weaved back and forth so that their paths intertwined, but they never touched.

There were thousands of them, and the longer Bowman stared, the more convinced he became that their motion was purposeful. They were too far away for him to make out any details of their structure; that he could see them at all in this colossal panorama meant that they must be scores—perhaps hundreds—of miles across. If they were organised entities, they were leviathans indeed, built to match the scale of the world they inhabited.

Perhaps they were only clouds of plasma, given temporary stability by some odd combination of natural forces—like the short-lived spheres of ball-lightning that still puzzled terrestrial scientists. That was an easy, and perhaps sooth-ing, explanation; but as Bowman looked down upon that star-wide streaming, he could not really believe it. Those glittering nodes of light *knew* where they were going; they were deliberately converging upon the pillar of fire raised by the White Dwarf as it orbited overhead.

Bowman stared once more at that ascending column, now marching along the horizon beneath the tiny, passive star that ruled it. Could it be pure imagination—or were there patches of brighter luminosity creeping up that great geyser of gas, as if myriads of shining sparks had combined into whole continents of phosphorescence?

The idea was almost beyond fantasy, but perhaps he was watching nothing less than a migration from star to star, across a bridge of fire. Whether it was a movement of mind-less, cosmic beasts driven across space by some lemming-like urge, or a vast concourse of intelligent entities, he would probably never know.

He was moving through a new order of creation, of which few men had ever dreamed. Beyond the realms of sea and land and air and space lay the realms of fire, which he alone had been privileged to glimpse. It was too much to expect that he would also understand.

44

Reception

The pillar of fire was marching over the edge of the sun, like a storm passing beyond the horizon. The scurrying flecks of light no longer moved across the redly-glowing starscape still thousands of miles below. Inside his space-pod, protected from an environment that could annihilate him within a millisecond, David Bowman awaited whatever had been prepared.

The White Dwarf was sinking fast as it hurtled along its orbit; presently it touched the horizon, set it aflame, and disappeared. A false twilight fell upon the inferno beneath, and in the sudden change of illumination, Bowman became aware that something was happening in the space around him.

The world of the red sun seemed to ripple, as if he was looking at it through running water. For a moment he wondered if this was some refractive effect, perhaps caused by the passage of an unusually violent shock-wave through the tortured atmosphere in which he was immersed.

The light was fading: it seemed that a second twilight was about to fall. Involuntarily, Bowman looked upwards, then checked himself sheepishly, as he remembered that here the main source of light was not the sky, but the blazing world below.

It seemed as if walls of some material like smoked glass were thickening around him, cutting out the red glow and obscuring the view. It became darker and darker; the faint roar of the stellar hurricanes also faded out. The space-pod was floating in silence, and in night. A moment later, there was the softest of bumps as it settled on some hard surface, and came to rest.

To rest on *what*? Bowman asked himself incredulously. Then light returned; and incredulity gave way to a heart-sinking despair—for as he saw what lay around him, he knew that he must be mad.

He was prepared, he thought, for any wonder. The only thing he had never expected was the utterly commonplace.

The space-pod was resting on the polished floor of an elegant, anonymous hotel suite that might have been in any large city on Earth. He was staring into a living-room with a coffee table, a divan, a dozen chairs, a writing desk, various lamps, a half-filled bookcase with some magazines lying on it, and even a bowl of flowers. Van Gogh's *Bridge at Arles* was hanging on one wall—Wyeth's *Christina's World* on another. He felt confident that when he pulled open the drawer of that desk he would find a Gideon Bible inside it....

If he was indeed mad, his delusions were beautifully organised. Everything was perfectly real; nothing vanished when he turned his back. The only incongruous element in the scene—and that certainly a major one—was the space-pod itself.

For many minutes, Bowman did not move from his seat. He half expected the vision around him to go away, but it remained as solid as anything he had ever seen in his life.

It *was* real—or else a phantom of the senses so superbly contrived that there was no way of distinguishing it from reality. Perhaps it was some kind of test; if so, not only his fate but that of the human race might well depend upon his actions in the next few minutes.

He could sit here and wait for something to happen, or he could open the pod and step outside to challenge the reality of the scene around him. The floor appeared to be solid; at least, it was bearing the weight of the space-pod. He was not likely to fall through it—whatever 'it' might really be.

But there was still the question of air; for all that he could tell, this room might be in vacuum, or might contain a poisonous atmosphere. He thought it very unlikely—no one would go to all this trouble without attending to such an essential detail—but he did not propose to take unnecessary risks. In any event, his years of training made him wary of contamination; he was reluctant to expose himself to an unknown environment, until he knew that there was no alternative. This place *looked* like a hotel room somewhere in the United States. That did not alter the fact that, in reality, he must be hundreds of light years from the Solar System.

He closed the helmet of his suit, sealing himself in, and actuated the hatch of the space-pod. There was a brief 'hiss' of pressure equalisation; then he stepped out into the room.

As far as he could tell, he was in a perfectly normal gravity field. He raised one arm, then let it fall freely. It flopped to his side in less than a second.

This made everything seem doubly unreal. Here he was wearing a spacesuit, standing—when he should have been floating—outside a vehicle which could only function properly in the absence of gravity. All his normal astronaut's reflexes were upset; he had to think before he made every movement.

Like a man in a trance, he walked slowly from his bare, unfurnished half of the room towards the hotel suite. It did not, as he had almost expected, disappear as he approached, but remained perfectly real—and apparently perfectly solid.

He stopped beside the coffee table. On it sat a conventional Bell System Picturephone, complete with the local directory. He bent down, and picked up the volume with his clumsy, gloved hands.

It bore, in the familiar type he had seen thousands of times, the name: WASHINGTON, D.C.

Then he looked more closely; and for the first time, he had objective proof that, although all this might be real, he was not on Earth.

He could read only the word WASHINGTON; the rest of the printing was a blur, as if it had been copied from a newspaper photograph. He opened the book at random and riffled through the pages. They were all blank sheets of crisp white material which was certainly not paper, though it looked very much like it.

He lifted the telephone receiver and pressed it against the plastic of his helmet. If there had been a dialling sound, he could have heard it through the conducting material. But, as he had expected, there was only silence.

So—it was all a fake, though a fantastically careful one. And it was clearly not intended to deceive but rather—he hoped—to reassure. That was a very comforting thought; nevertheless he would not remove his suit until he had completed his voyage of exploration.

All the furniture seemed sound and solid enough; he tried the chairs, and they supported his weight. But the drawers in the desk would not open; they were dummies.

So were the books and magazines; like the telephone directory, only the titles were readable. They formed an odd selection—mostly rather trashy best-sellers, a few sensational works of non-fiction, and some well-publicised autobiographies. There was nothing less than three years old, and little of any intellectual content. Not that it mattered, for the books could not even be taken down from the shelves.

There were two doors that opened readily enough. The first one took him into a small but comfortable bedroom, fitted with bed, bureau, two chairs, light switches that actually worked, and a clothes closet. He opened this, and found himself looking at four suits, a dressing gown, a dozen white shirts, and several sets of underwear, all neatly draped from hangers.

He took down one of the suits, and inspected it carefully. As far as his gloved hands could judge, it was made of material that was more like fur than wool. It was also a little out of style; on Earth, no one had been wearing single-breasted suits for at least four years.

Next to the bedroom was a bathroom, complete with fittings which, he was relieved to note, were not dummies, but worked in a perfectly normal manner. And after that was a kitchenette, with electric cooker, ice-box, storage cupboards, crockery and cutlery, sink, table and chairs. Bowman began to explore this not only with curiosity, but with mounting hunger.

First he opened the ice-box, and a wave of cold mist rolled out. The shelves were well-stocked with packages and cans, all of them looking perfectly familiar from a distance, though at close quarters their proprietary labels were blurred and unreadable. However, there was a notable absence of eggs, milk, butter, meat, fruit, or any other unprocessed food; the ice-box held only items that had already been packaged in some way.

Bowman picked up a carton of a familiar breakfast cereal, thinking as he did so that it was odd to keep this frozen. The moment he lifted the package, he knew that it certainly did *not* contain cornflakes; it was much too heavy.

He ripped open the lid, and examined the contents. The box contained a slightly moist blue substance, of about the weight and texture of bread pudding. Apart from its odd colour, it looked quite appetising.

But this is ridiculous, Bowman told himself. I am almost certainly being watched, and I must look an idiot wearing this suit. If this is some kind of intelligence test, I've probably failed already.

Without further hesitation, he walked back into the bedroom and began to undo the clamp of his helmet. When it was loose, he lifted the helmet a fraction of an inch, cracked the seal, and took a cautious sniff. As far as he could tell, he was breathing perfectly normal air.

He dropped the helmet on the bed, and began thankfully —and rather stiffly—to divest himself of his suit. When he had finished, he stretched, took a few deep breaths, and carefully hung the spacesuit up among the more conventional articles of clothing in the closet. It looked rather odd there, but the compulsive tidiness that Bowman shared with all astronauts would never have allowed him to leave it anywhere else.

Then he walked quickly back into the kitchen, and began to inspect the 'cereal' box at closer quarters.

The blue bread pudding had a faint, spicy smell, something like a macaroon. Bowman weighed it in his hand, then broke off a piece and cautiously sniffed at it. Though he felt sure now that there would be no deliberate attempt to poison him, there was always the possibility of mistakes—especially in a matter so complex as biochemistry.

He nibbled at a few crumbs, then chewed and swallowed the fragment of food; it was excellent, though the flavour was so elusive as to be almost indescribable. If he closed his eyes, he could imagine it was meat, or wholemeal bread, or even dried fruit. Unless there were unexpected after-effects, he had nothing to fear from starvation.

When he had eaten just a few mouthfuls of the substance, and already felt quite satisfied, he looked for something to drink. There were half a dozen cans of beer—again of a famous brand—at the back of the ice-box, and he pressed the tab on one of them to open it.

The pre-stressed metal lid popped off along its strain lines, exactly as usual. But the can did not contain beer; to Bowman's surprised disappointment, it held more of the blue food.

In a few seconds he had opened half a dozen of the other packages and cans. Whatever their labels, their contents were the same; it seemed that his diet was going to be a little monotonous, and that he would have nothing but water to drink. He filled a glass from the kitchen faucet, and sipped at it cautiously.

He spat out the first few drops at once; the taste was terrible. Then, rather ashamed of his instinctive reaction, he forced himself to drink the rest.

That first sip had been enough to identify the liquid. It tasted terrible because it had no taste at all; the faucet was supplying pure, distilled water. His unknown hosts were obviously taking no chances with his health.

Feeling much refreshed, he then had a quick shower. There was no soap, which was another minor inconvenience, but there was a very efficient hot-air drier in which he luxuriated for a while before trying on underpants, vest and dressing gown from the clothes closet. After that, he laid down on the bed, stared up at the ceiling, and tried to make sense of this fantastic situation.

He had made little progress when he was distracted by another line of thought. Immediately above the bed was the usual hotel-type ceiling TV screen; he had assumed that, like the telephone and books, it was a dummy.

But the control unit on its swinging bedside arm looked so realistic that he could not resist playing with it; and as his fingers touched the ON sensor disc, the screen lit up.

Feverishly, he started to tap out channel selector codes at random, and almost at once he got his first picture.

It was a well-known African news commentator, discussing the attempts being made to preserve the last remnants of his country's wild life. Bowman listened for a few seconds, so captivated by the sound of a human voice that he did not in the least care what it was talking about. Then he changed channels.

In the next five minutes, he got a symphony orchestra playing Walton's Violin Concerto, a discussion on the sad state of the legitimate theatre, a western, a demonstration of a new headache cure, a panel game in some oriental language, a psychodrama, three news commentaries, a football game, a lecture on solid geometry (in Russian) and several tuning signals and data transmissions. It was, in fact, a perfectly normal selection from the world's TV programmes, and apart from the psychological uplift it gave him, it confirmed one suspicion that had already been forming in his mind.

All the programmes were about two years old. That was around the time T.M.A.-1 had been discovered, and it was hard to believe that this was a pure coincidence. *Something* had been monitoring the radio waves; that ebon block had been busier than Man had suspected.

He continued to wander across the spectrum, and suddenly recognised a familiar scene. Here was this very suite, now occupied by a celebrated actor who was furiously denouncing an unfaithful mistress. Bowman looked with a shock of recognition upon the living-room he had just left —and when the camera followed the indignant couple towards the bedroom, he involuntarily looked towards the door to see if anyone was entering.

So that was how this reception area had been prepared for him; his hosts had based their ideas of terrestrial living upon TV programmes. His feeling that he was inside a movie set was almost literally true.

He had learned all that he wished to for the moment, and turned off the set. What do I do now? he asked himself, locking his fingers behind his head and staring at the blank screen.

He was physically and emotionally exhausted, yet it seemed impossible that one could sleep, in such fantastic surroundings, and further from Earth than any man in history had ever been. But the comfortable bed, and the instinctive wisdom of the body, conspired together against his will.

He fumbled for the light switch, and the room was plunged into darkness. Within seconds, he had passed beyond the reach of dreams.

So, for the last time, David Bowman slept.

45

Recapitulation

There being no further use for it, the furniture of the suite dissolved back into the mind of its creator. Only the bed remained—and the walls, shielding this fragile organism from the energies it could not yet control.

In his sleep, David Bowman stirred restlessly. He did not wake, nor did he dream, but he was no longer wholly unconscious. Like a fog creeping through a forest, something invaded his mind. He sensed it only dimly, for the full impact would have destroyed him as surely as the fires raging beyond these walls. Beneath that dispassionate scrutiny, he felt neither hope nor fear; all emotion had been leached away.

He seemed to be floating in free space, while around him stretched, in all directions, an infinite geometrical grid of dark lines or threads, along which moved tiny nodes of light—some slowly, some at dazzling speed. Once he had peered through a microscope at a cross-section of a human brain, and in its network of nerve-fibres had glimpsed the same labyrinthine complexity. But that had been dead and static, whereas this transcended life itself. He knew—or believed he knew—that he was watching the operation of some gigantic mind, contemplating the universe of which he was so tiny a part.

The vision, or illusion, lasted only a moment. Then the crystalline planes and lattices, and the interlocking perspectives of moving light flickered out of existence, as David Bowman moved into a realm of consciousness that no man had ever experienced before.

At first, it seemed that Time itself was running backwards. Even this marvel he was prepared to accept, before he realised the subtler truth.

The springs of memory were being tapped; in controlled recollection he was reliving the past. There was the hotel suite—there the space-pod—there the burning starscapes of the red sun—there the shining core of the galaxy—there the gateway through which he had re-emerged into the universe. And not only vision, but all the sense impressions, and all the emotions he had felt at the time, were racing past, more and more swiftly. His life was unreeling like a tape-recorder playing back at ever-increasing speed.

Now he was once more aboard *Discovery*, and the rings of Saturn filled the sky. Before that, he was repeating his final dialogue with Hal; he was seeing Frank Poole leave on his last mission; he was hearing the voice of Earth, assuring him that all was well.

And even as he relived these events, he knew that all indeed was well. He was retrogressing down the corridors of time, being drained of knowledge and experience as he swept back towards his childhood. But nothing was being lost; all that he had ever been, at every moment of his life, was being transferred to safer keeping. Even as one David Bowman ceased to exist, another became immortal.

Faster, faster, he moved back into forgotten years, and into a simpler world. Faces he had once loved, and had thought lost beyond recall, smiled at him sweetly. He smiled back with fondness, and without pain.

Now, at last, the headlong regression was slackening; the wells of memory were nearly dry. Time flowed more and more sluggishly, approaching a moment of stasis—as a swinging pendulum, at the limit of its arc, seems frozen for one eternal instant, before the next cycle begins.

The timeless instant passed; the pendulum reversed its swing. In an empty room, floating amid the fires of a double star twenty thousand light-years from Earth, a baby opened its eyes and began to cry.

46

Transformation

Then it became silent, as it saw that it was no longer alone.

A ghostly, glimmering rectangle had formed in the empty air. It solidified into a crystal tablet, lost its transparency, and became suffused with a pale, milky luminescence. Tantalising, ill-defined phantoms moved across its surface and in its depths. They coalesced into bars of light and shadow, then formed intermeshing, spoked patterns that began slowly to rotate, in time with the pulsing rhythm that now seemed to fill the whole of space.

It was a spectacle to grasp and hold the attention of any child—or of any man-ape. But, as it had been three million years before, it was only the outward manifestation of forces too subtle to be consciously perceived. It was merely a toy to distract the senses, while the real processing was carried out at far deeper levels of the mind.

This time, the processing was swift and certain, as the new design was woven. For in the aeons since their last meeting, much had been learned by the weaver; and the material on which he practised his art was now of an infinitely finer texture. But whether it should be permitted to form part of his still-growing tapestry, only the future could tell.

With eyes that already held more than human intentness, the baby stared into the depths of the crystal monolith, seeing—but not yet understanding—the mysteries that lay beyond. It knew that it had come home, that here was the origin of many races beside his own; but it knew also that it could not stay. Beyond this moment lay another birth, stranger than any in the past.

Now the moment had come; the glowing patterns no longer echoed the secrets in the crystal's heart. As they died, so too the protective walls faded back into the non-existence from which they had briefly emerged, and the red sun filled the sky.

The metal and plastic of the forgotten space-pod, and the clothing once worn by an entity who had called himself David Bowman, flashed into flame. The last links with Earth were gone, resolved back into their component atoms.

But the child scarcely noticed, as he adjusted himself to the comfortable glow of his new environment. He still needed, for a little while, this shell of matter as the focus of his powers. His indestructible body was his mind's present image of itself; and for all his powers, he knew that he was still a baby. So he would remain until he had decided on a new form, or had passed beyond the necessities of matter.

And now it was time to go—though in one sense he would never leave this place where he had been re-born, for he would always be part of the entity that used this double star for its unfathomable purposes. The direction, though not the nature, of his destiny was clear before him, and there was no need to trace the devious path by which he had come. With the instincts of three million years, he now perceived that there were more ways than one behind the back of space. The ancient mechanisms of the Star Gate had served him well, but he would not need them again.

The glimmering rectangular shape that had once seemed no more than a slab of crystal still floated before him, indifferent as he was to the harmless flames of the inferno beneath. It encapsulated yet unfathomed secrets of space and time, but some at least he now understood and was able to command. How obvious—how *necessary*—was that mathematical ratio of its sides, the quadratic sequence 1 :4 :9! And how naive to have imagined that the series ended at this point, in only three dimensions!

He focussed his mind upon these geometrical simplicities,

and as his thoughts brushed against it, the empty framework filled with the darkness of the interstellar night. The glow of the red sun faded—or, rather, seemed to recede in all directions at once; and there before him was the luminous whirlpool of the Galaxy.

It might have been some beautiful, incredibly detailed model, embedded in a block of plastic. But it was the reality, grasped as a whole with senses now more subtle than vision. If he wished, he could focus his attention upon any one of its hundred billion stars: and he could do much more than that.

Here he was, adrift in this great river of suns, halfway between the banked fires of the galactic core and the lonely, scattered sentinel stars of the rim. And *here* he wished to be, on the far side of this chasm in the sky, this serpentine band of darkness, empty of all stars. He knew that this formless chaos, visible only by the glow that limned its edges from fire-mists far beyond, was the still unused stuff of creation, the raw material of evolutions yet to be. Here, Time had not begun; not until the suns that now burned were long since dead, would light and life reshape this void.

Unwittingly, he had crossed it once: now he must cross it again—this time, under his own volition. The thought filled him with a sudden, freezing terror, so that for a moment he was wholly disorientated, and his new vision of the universe trembled and threatened to shatter into a thousand fragments.

It was not fear of the galactic gulfs that chilled his soul, but a more profound disquiet, stemming from the unborn future. For he had left behind the time-scales of his human origin; now, as he contemplated that band of starless night, he knew his first intimations of the Eternity that yawned before him.

Then he remembered that he would never be alone, and his panic slowly ebbed The crystal-clear perception of the universe was restored to him—not, he knew, wholly by his own efforts. When he needed guidance in his first faltering steps, it would be there.

Confident once more, like a high-diver who had regained his nerve, he launched himself across the light-years. The Galaxy burst forth from the mental frame in which he had enclosed it; stars and nebulae poured past him in an illusion of infinite speed. Phantom suns exploded and fell behind as he slipped like a shadow through their cores; the cold, dark waste of cosmic dust which he had once feared seemed no more than the beat of a raven's wing across the face of the sun.

The stars were thinning out; the glare of the Milky Way was dimming into a pale ghost of the glory he had known— and, when he was ready, would know again.

He was back, precisely where he wished to be, in the space that men called real.

47

Star-Child

There before him, a glittering toy no Star-Child could resist, floated the planet Earth with all its peoples.

He had returned in time. Down there on that crowded globe, the alarms would be flashing across the radar screens, the great tracking telescopes would be searching the skies— and history as men knew it would be drawing to a close.

A thousand miles below, he became aware that a slumbering cargo of death had awoken, and was stirring sluggishly in its orbit. The feeble energies it contained were no possible menace to him; but he preferred a cleaner sky. He put forth his will, and the circling megatons flowered in a silent detonation that brought a brief, false dawn to half the sleeping globe.

Then he waited, marshalling his thoughts and brooding over his still untested powers. For though he was master of the world, he was not quite sure what to do next.

But he would think of something.